TRAIL OF THE OENT'RFAZR

TRAIL OF THE OENT'RFAZR

LARRY ELLIS

TRAIL OF THE OENT'RFAZR

iUniverse books may be ordered through booksellers or by contacting:

iUniverse
1663 Liberty Drive
Bloomington, IN 47403
www.iuniverse.com
1-800-Authors (1-800-288-4677)

Because of the dynamic nature of the Internet, any web addresses or links contained in this book may have changed since publication and may no longer be valid. The views expressed in this work are solely those of the author and do not necessarily reflect the views of the publisher, and the publisher hereby disclaims any responsibility for them.

Any people depicted in stock imagery provided by Thinkstock are models, and such images are being used for illustrative purposes only. Certain stock imagery © Thinkstock.

ISBN: 978-1-4917-7513-4 (sc)
ISBN: 978-1-4917-7512-7 (e)

Library of Congress Control Number: 2015913477

Print information available on the last page.

iUniverse rev. date: 11/12/2015

Contents

Prologue vii

Breakthrough 2010 1

Hunter 7

First Contact 9

The Word List 13

The Journey Begins 20

Lupton 24

Navajo Springs 31

The Lost Village 41

Barringer 52

Two Guns 66

Zoo 78

An Early Breakfast 90

Lava River Caves 94

Dante 105

The Caverns 119

A Way Out 136

Mercury 150

Atomic Bombs 165

UFO Cave 177

Oatman 185

Goldfish Confrontation 193

Aftermath 198

Prologue

News Flash, WHJB Radio, December 9, 1965
Kecksburg, Pennsylvania

In 1897, science fiction master H. G. Wells described an incredibly violent war with an invading army of grotesque Martians that sought to obliterate the entire human race with their heat rays and three-legged, metal monsters of death. In 1938, Orson Welles broadcast the story of that same Martian attack on the radio on what would become the scariest and deadliest Halloween eve in our history. Today, we witnessed the opening of what may become the real war of the worlds.

This is Christopher Ray, WHJB radio in Kecksburg, Pennsylvania, broadcasting from north of town. Reports are coming in from all over the country that a flying saucer has crashed close to where I am now standing. Eyewitnesses described a fireball moving across Ohio and Pennsylvania skies, which, according to some observers, seemed to be under intelligent control. When the craft reached an area above our small town of Kecksburg, it emitted a pulsing blue light, made a sweeping turn, and then appeared to free fall from the sky and crash into our woods.

It took the army just thirty minutes to reach the crash site and, as soon as they arrived, they quarantined the woods, effectively preventing anyone from entering or leaving the area. Those people who were already in the area were arrested. However, this reporter talked to Heather Romero, a local Kecksburg Girl Scout leader, who had been camping near the crash site and was trying to home before the army arrived. She told us that she saw a shadowy figure struggle to get out of the saucer seconds after it crashed, move quickly away, and then stop and climb a tree. It was only in the tree for a few seconds and then it jumped down and disappeared into the woods. I asked her if she knew why the thing had stopped to climb the tree and she said no. When asked about the shadowy figure, she said that it stood upright like a human, was as tall as a human, and moved like a human on two legs but she couldn't see any specific features.

When I asked her about the UFO itself, she replied, "The crashed saucer was bronze colored, acorn-shaped about ten feet tall and about five feet around with a wide bumper at the bottom which was covered with colored symbols and figures that appeared to be some kind of hieroglyphics."

Wait, it looks like the army is pushing everyone further away from the site. I hear a diesel engine starting just over the hill where the crash occurred. Now, I see a flatbed trailer moving slowly away from the site. It is hauling a large, pointed object covered with a tarp and is surrounded by a number of soldiers prominently displaying rifles and side arms. The army appears to be widening the perimeter around the crash site so …

Ladies and gentlemen, I don't believe this. I'm now being told by a large soldier with a larger rifle to sign off the air now and that, if I don't, I will be placed in military custody and shot.

I will be on the air later to bring more of this story to you but for right now, this is the 'Big Dawg' himself, WHJB's own Christopher Ray, saying, 'Look out for the Martians…but be afraid of the military.'

Breakthrough 2010

Hunter stared at the headline under the picture on the wall. *Man's Brain Dissolves During Time Travel Experiment.*

One of the reporters noticed the direction of his gaze. "Are you concerned about that happening to you, Dr. Johnson?"

Before he could answer, another reporter cut in. "Are you ready to make history, Dr. Johnson?"

These questions sound almost meaningless, Hunter thought. As he lay on the gurney, waiting for the IV to be plugged into his arm, he reflected on the article that the *Arizona Sun* published that morning.

> October 8, 2010, may prove to be a significant date in the history of the town of Globe, Arizona. For over a decade now, Dr. Hunter Johnson and his team of talented researchers at INTERfaz's Old Dominion mine, located in this small southeast Arizona town, have worked diligently to prepare for man's next attempt at time travel. Cecilia Marie, INTERfaz's CEO, told reporters, "Johnson's incredible ability to see and understand the complex inter-relationships of the philosophical, mathematical, and chemical abstractions needed for time travel was a key to being ready to break the *future* barrier." Using thought amplification stimulation, a hyper-potent cocktail of DNA chemical derivatives developed by Johnson and his wife, and a lava formation called a tube, Johnson is now preparing to become the world's first successful time traveler.

"Hum," Hunter remarked, as his focus returned to the present. "It seems like they expect something important to happen here today." He watched as the covey of reporters left the experiment room. The mixture of the smell of fresh paint and the pungent odor of disinfectant caused many of the observers in the room to gag. A large array of screens and monitors covering the back wall blinked in a symphony of rainbow-flavored text.

"This place looks like an advertisement for a new Crayola Crayons product," Hunter told his assistant. The back wall looked like an oversized electronics store display compared to the front wall, which featured only a singular phrase in large, boldly printed letters: *ANY SUFFICIENTLY ADVANCED TECHNOLOGY IS INDISTINGUISHABLE FROM MAGIC.*

"Did you do the final calibration on the recording equipment?" Hunter queried his assistant.

"For the tenth time, Doc, yeah, I did."

Then, without warning, a death-like pall settled over the room.

Hunter glanced around at all the people in the room. "Why is it so quiet? Did I already travel into the future and no one bothered to say 'Welcome back'?"

The door screeched metal against metal as it opened, and a nurse wearing a starched, light blue uniform with the INTERfaz insignia on her cap and collar entered enter the room. She was carrying a tray that held an IV bottle of purple liquid, plastic tubing, and a syringe that looked like it belonged in an elephant compound. Hunter stared at her nametag and did a double take.

"Does that say … Oy, it does …," Hunter groaned. "Nurse Ratched." She glared at him with no hint of a smile and hung up the IV bottle containing the purple chemicals that would shortly send him into the future.

Seeing the IV bottle hanging there as a sign of what was to come prompted Hunter to quip, "Uh oh, make it a double, would you, barkeep?"

Nurse Ratched reached for the other end of the IV tube and inserted it into Hunter's arm. She checked it twice and then opened the drain block. All eyes in the room focused on the IV tubing as the liquid slowly formed one drop, then two, then three finally merging into a continuous, purple stream. The purple stream flowed lazily down the tubing and disappeared into Hunt's arm.

Watching the liquid disappear, Hunter announced in a slightly uneven manner, "All right, here we go." He whispered to his wife standing next to him, "I love you, Doris." Hearing that nickname said out loud reminded Hunter of the first time he saw her at the U of A. Margie was almost six feet tall with blonde hair that she'd worn in pigtails then. Her face was dotted with a crop of golden freckles that immediately changed whatever season it was into summer. With her sparkling, azure blue eyes, blonde pigtails, and those freckles, she was the quintessential girl next door. So much so, that Hunter would continually ask her, "Are you really Doris Day?" It had been the beginning of what would be a special relationship and an endearing nickname.

"Hunter? Are you all right?"

Hunter nodded and commented in an ever-softening voice, "Let's get this show on the road." He grew very quiet as the IV began to take effect but he was conscious enough to give a final thumbs-up sign to all the team members.

"Watch his eyelids," Hunter's assistant told everyone. When most of the IV had drained into his arm, Hunter's muscles relaxed perceptibly, and he got very still. His eyes opened wide one last time and then closed. The digital readouts turned a fiery red and alarms announced a slowing in Hunt's major body functions.

A member of the team called out, "05:29:30 In transition." Several people jumped at the suddenness of the sound. However, most just watched the readouts in silence.

Almost before anyone could comment, the same voice called out, "He's on his way back." The raucous blare of the alarms dissipated into nothingness as the digital numbers tracking Hunt's vital signs returned to their normal rainbow hues. This was the point in the previous experiment where something had gone horribly wrong but no one said anything this time.

Hunter's eyes opened. "Anybody see where I went or if I came back?"

As murmurs of laughter spread among the staff, the same faceless voice called out, "05:30:00 Out transition." Hunter had been gone for a total of thirty seconds. A buzz passed through the room as team members realized the experiment had not failed, and their leader was physically and mentally fine.

Hunt touched his head. "Can someone get me an aspirin…and a scotch? Wait, never mind the aspirin."

Nurse Ratched began disconnecting the IV so that the medical team could move Hunt.

When she was done, she admonished the medical team sternly, "Get him away from me but don't get too close. He bites." Her mouth curled up at the ends as she watched the staff come to Hunter. The medical staff, who had been intently scouring the electronic read-outs for any sign of an anomaly, started wheeling him toward the temporary infirmary for a quick medical check.

Hunter addressed the group in the main room as he was rolling towards the door, "I think I am in one piece. Why don't all of you go have a beer while the shrinks figure out if everything that left with me came back with me?"

The medical staff rolled him into the infirmary and moved to their positions around the room. The head of the medical team stood near Hunter's gurney and asked the usual how are you feeling now questions.

"How do you feel now compared to how you felt during transition?"

Hunt sat up on his elbows. "Shortly after I was given the 'juice', I began feeling slightly lost and disoriented and then suddenly everything cleared. When it did, I saw … no, that's not right. I became conscious of the town of Globe and I saw a newspaper headline dated three days from now that read 'Car Crash Kills 4' and then I heard that there was a fire in the high school gym."

When he was told he touched his head after he returned, Hunter replied, "I do remember feeling a bit of pain in my temple." Then he was quiet for a few seconds. "Just before I became aware of the events I described, I experienced a sort of sensory freeze where I couldn't move or feel anything. I could still see things but it was like being in a photograph until the pain began in my temple. That pain subsided as the sensory freeze ended. That same pain was what I felt after I returned." The doctors and psychologists agreed for now that it was probably a reaction to the DNA chemicals but they would do some extensive testing later to confirm it.

After the evaluation session was completed, INTERfaz's PR office released the following announcement:

At approximately 5:29:30 this morning, October 8, 2010, Dr. Hunter Johnson, the Director of INTERfaz's R and D program, transported into the future. When he returned, he brought back two pieces of information about things that were going to happen on October 11, three days from today. There will be a fire in the high school gym and four people will be killed in an automobile accident. Until his trip is validated on October 11, Dr. Johnson is resting and undergoing de-briefing.

◆━◈━◆

Hunter had come to work early to allow himself time to write his official report on the experiment while the day was still quiet. Today was the eleventh and he, like most of the staff at the office, was anxiously awaiting the first news of the day. He heard a noise outside his office and got up from his desk. He went to his office window and saw a large number of the INTERfaz staff milling around the front door waiting for the paper. When it was delivered, a staffer opened it. Hunter opened the window to listen. "Car Crash Kills Four- Johnson for Real." Hunter smiled and made a confirming fist.

Then he heard the emergency sirens and saw the diesel powered fire trucks headed down the street in the direction of the high school. The staffers turned around, focused on Hunter standing in his office window, and began to applaud and cheer. Just like that, Hunter was anointed as the world's first confirmed time traveler.

Later, as he sat quietly at his desk thinking about the events of the past three days, he realized that time travel was going to be long-term reality and he began to ask himself some pointed life questions. Will I be able to get back to the present time, if I travel too far into the future? Will I be able to travel into the past and the future? Will it change me physically or mentally? Will the Rogers-Soltys Paradox affect my observations? Will Einstein's theory of relativity apply to me? Will Scotty and Margie be affected? And, most important, will I still like Big Macs? He chuckled momentarily at his last question and then his face morphed into a cross between extreme fear and confused uncertainty. He stared at his arm where the IV had been inserted.

I wonder? Did I just give birth to a caterpillar or a butterfly?

Hunter

Hunter sat on his front porch taking in the serenity of the mountains in the softening twilight. The quiet of the evening magnified the sound of his breathing. He reached down and scratched Bill along the length of his back. Bill was the family basset hound who was Hunter's constant companion and confidant.

"What a rat race this has been but I don't think history will forget us very soon," Hunter told Bill, who nuzzled his head under Hunt's hand. "But, regardless of how significant it all is, I'm glad to be out of it and back home where I belong."

Just two weeks had elapsed since the world found out that he was the first successful time traveler but what a time those two weeks had been. Unending interview requests, incessant phone calls, maddening requests for autographs even in restrooms, not to mention the trumped-up television appearances, the myriad of debriefing sessions asking the same questions over and over, lecture requests for any meeting anywhere blurred the days. But, most of all, he decried the lack of time to just relax, like this. Well, not exactly like this. He sat on his porch on nights like this for many years and he always came away relaxed and recharged. But tonight … tonight was different.

I can't shake the feeling that something bad is going to happen. To make things worse, his head throbbed with one of those Kecksburg headaches, as he called them. He tried to work around the uncomfortable feelings as he usually did by remembering things about his mom and dad and school with Margie.

Funny, I haven't thought about my real parents in many years. It always bothered him that he could never find out anything about them. Every record he checked ended in a dead end. It was as if they didn't exist or were aliens, who had suddenly returned to their home planet.

"I can just see my folks circling Saturn in a spaceship." Then, he thought about the University of Arizona, where two of the best things in his life happened. It was there in a lab, after one of his killer headaches and a meeting with that strange Dr. Mern, that he stumbled on a breakthrough formula that opened up the potential for time travel. It would ultimately lead to his doctorate and his worldwide reputation in the field. He remembered how strange Mern's eyes were. Then his thoughts turned to other best thing to come out of the U of A–Margie. They were physically and emotionally well-matched when they met. Hunter was a lanky six feet four inches tall with short brown hair that was giving way to a growing bald spot, a thick handlebar moustache, and ears that stuck out like the doors on a taxicab. Margie never let him forget about his ears.

During the last month of school, Hunter had cornered her at Old Main Fountain and confessed, "I don't know how serious you are about me, but I definitely want us to get very serious in our relationship." Hunter waited for an answer. Then, he saw her blue eyes twinkle as they always did when she was getting ready to zing him.

Oh no, she thinks I'm kidding and here comes one of her Saturday night specials. But then she'd stepped forward and pulled his face to hers and hung one on him. Every muscle and nerve in his face tingled uncontrollably and then went numb. She focused her shimmering, blue eyes on his as she pulled back from the kiss.

"I didn't kiss you because I think you're the sexiest man alive ... well, actually I did, but I wanted you to know how happy I am you want that because it's what I want too." Hunter touched his lips, remembering the fire that kiss had ignited in his whole body.

I had to have intense medical care on both my lips for weeks to try to save them after that kiss. God, I can still feel it after all these years. He smiled at the thought.

First Contact

A sudden noise brought Hunter back into the present.

What the heck was that? It required a few seconds for him to remember where he was and that the noise was his phone ringing. He stood, walked quickly into the house, and then headed into the family room where the phone was.

"All right, hold your horses." As he walked towards the phone, he noticed the phantom sensation he'd experienced on the porch seemed to have intensified. As he entered the family room, his eyes focused on the framed piece of silver metal he'd found imbedded in a tree at the 1965 crash site. It had a pale blue inverted triangle with an offset, irregular orange circle on it.

What are you and what is there about you that are so important? he thought to himself for the hundredth time.

Hunter picked up the phone. "Hello."

Out of a background of silence, a reedy, metallic voice spoke, "Dr. Johnson?"

"Yes. This is Dr. Johnson."

"Prepare for your journey." Silence followed the single sentence and then a short crackle of static burst on the line.

"What?" "Hello?" "Hello?" Hunter put the phone down and, after several moments of thought, decided the call was a prank resulting from all the publicity from his time travels. He walked quietly into his bedroom and lay down gently so as not to awaken Margie. Within moments, he'd fallen asleep.

At exactly 2:20 a.m., Hunt bolted upright, gasping for breath, sweating, and shivering all at the same time.

"What's wrong with me?" He tried to control his shaking and catch his breath so as not to wake his wife.

In a voice softened by sleep, Margie questioned, "What is it, babe?"

"I just had the wildest dream. I was standing in an open field, observing the night sky. There were dozens of 'things' floating around. They all seemed to be staring at me as if they knew something I didn't. They didn't say anything but their expressions seemed to change into ones of sadness. Then, they all folded up, encased themselves in purple liquid cocoons, and spelled out the word *journey*. Then, they vanished."

"Purple cocoons?"

"Yeah, and right after that, I woke up hearing echoes of the word."

Margie looked at her husband. "That is one of the strangest dreams you ever had."

Hunter nodded his head. "I haven't had intense dreams like that since ... since Kecksburg." By now, his hands had stopped shaking. He sat for a few minutes thinking about the dream and then lay back down. He tossed and turned for half an hour before falling back into a deep sleep.

He awoke the next morning refreshed. The uncomfortable feeling had vanished, but he still had one of his Kecksburg headaches. He got up, dressed, and mowed and edged the lawn before it got too warm.

When he was done, he went into the kitchen and poured himself a glass of lemonade. He was relaxing in the kitchen thinking about what had happened earlier that morning when his son, Scott, came in and got himself a glass of cold water.

Scott must have sensed something was not right. "What's wrong, Pop? You look worried."

Hunter told him about the strange telephone call. "Any other time, I would have forgotten it but, for some reason, I can't stop wondering about the message."

Scott listened. "Wow, that's something. Are you sure someone wasn't just playing a prank?"

"I wish I knew, Scotty. I wish I knew."

Scott watched his dad for several minutes and then began "All right, I've given you plenty of time to rest. It's time for me to take you outside and kick your skinny butt ... again."

A wisp of a smile crossed Hunter's face. "Hold-up, I need to finish my 'ade. That should give you enough time to call four of your friends, your really big friends, to help you accomplish that task. You're gonna need lots of help." He tried his best to sound menacing but he knew exactly what was going to happen to him.

Changing topics, Hunter posed one of his favorite questions. "How're your Arizona history classes going at school?"

"You know, Dad, it was really incredible in my classes. Every time we talked about any of the places where you and I had camped out when I was little, I could remember touching something at the site. When I heard the professor talk about it, I remembered what it felt like. It was—"

"Like you traveled back in time?"

"Yeah, exactly. What do you think caused that, Pop?"

"Do you remember the Star Trek Next Generation movie *First Contact*? The scene where Data and Picard have gone back in time to the first warp event and they are seeing the Phoenix in person. Data is watching Picard touch the ship with his eyes closed and asks him what he's doing. Picard tells him that he must've seen the ship hundreds of times in the Smithsonian but he was never able to touch it. Then Data asks if touching altered the perception of the Phoenix? Picard told him that for humans, touch can connect them to an object in a very personal way and make it seem more real."

"I think I understand," Scott reflected.

The two went outside where Scott picked up an errant basketball and the two men started their semi-weekly workout on the makeshift basketball court in the backyard. Scott was six inches taller than Hunt and well muscled from years of almost continuous ball playing. Hunt was no slouch with the round ball but he couldn't hold his own with his son. Not only was he tall, Scott had cat-like reflexes and agility uncommon in tall people. Hunter tried his best but Scott dunked the ball repeatedly at will over and around his dad.

Finally, Scott couldn't contain himself. "Are we about done? I don't want to make you late for your meeting of the National Organization of Leprechauns or was that the Arizona Homunculus Club?" Hunt laughed as he watched Scott work his magic with the round ball and complete the day's *fait accompli.*

Scott grabbed the ball, wiped it on his leg, and smiled, "Gonna set this aside for more punishment later."

The Word List

Margie looked outside and called, "Dinner, you two." Father and son came in and sat down at the table. It was a bit old-fashioned, but evenings when the three of them could be together like this were a favorite time for Hunter. Margie had made her special enchilada-peanut butter soufflé, which Hunter and Scott devoured each time she served it.

Margie glanced at both of them. "How did your ball game go, guys?" knowing exactly what the answer was.

Hunt responded with a straight face. "Really close couple of games."

"Pop is getting better. This time he started driving for the hoop from the top of the key and didn't need oxygen by the time he got the lay-up...oops, the almost lay-up."

Margie smiled at Scott and then patted her husband's arm in a there–there manner.

After scarfing down his last bite of soufflé, Scott announced, "I'm gonna transfer to a school nearer here so I can come home when you cook this stuff, Mom."

Hunter saw his chance and wasn't going to miss it. "I don't think so. We want you out of here so we don't have to listen to you belch and pass gas every forty-five minutes when you go into the kitchen to get something to eat. Maybe mom won't have to go shopping five times a week to keep the refrigerator full. By the way, I had lunch with Anthony Romero, the new owner of the Fry's grocery store."

Margie exhaled so Hunter could hear her. "Now what are you telling people about Scott?"

Hunter ignored his wife. "Your eating habits are so well known around here he suggested we consider just having your food delivered directly to our house. He would leave the delivery trucks here so we could use them as outside pantries."

Scott just stared at his dad.

"That would save them the time it takes to unload the food, check it, stock it, and load it through their inventory system, and then to ring it out at the register. And I, for one, am tired of never being to find anything to eat in this house." He feigned disbelief. "It's like living with an oversized goat."

Scott reached over, picked up his mom's entire cheesecake, put it on his plate, covered it with his hands, and then bleated at his dad.

Hunter stared at his laughing wife. "See what I mean?"

After they finished dinner, Hunter cleared the table and then went into the living room to watch TV. Scott was already there.

"What're ya reading, kid?"

"I found a new book called *Pioneers of Forever* about time travel, and it even mentions you."

"What does it say?"

"Dr. Johnson's successes are due to the great intelligence of his handsome and sexy son, who tells his dad how to time travel as he kicks his butt on the basketball court."

Scott ducked the pillow his dad threw at him.

When Margie joined them, Hunt hugged her. "I think I'm going to bed."

"Too much basketball for you, Pop?"

"When pigs fly." Hunter smiled, "Night, punk."

"Night, old man."

Hunt headed toward the bedroom and got undressed. He picked up the manuscript of the experiment and lay down. After an hour or so of reading, he yawned, put the notes down, and turned out the lights.

At exactly 2:20 a.m., Hunt screamed.

"LEAX." He yelled repeating the word he'd heard in his dream.

This time Margie was fully awake. "Hunter, what happened?"

"It was the same dream as last night. Except this time the final word was different."

"I heard you yell something that sounded like leaks. Was that it?"

"It was LEAX," Hunter responded.

"The strange dream seems to get stranger," Margie commented as she lay back down on the bed.

Hunter turned on the table lamp, grabbed the pencil and pad there, and wrote 'Journey' and 'LEAX' on the pad.

He stared at the words on the paper. "What the heck is a LEAX anyway?" He continued looking at the words for several more seconds and then put the pencil and pad down, turned out the light, and, in a short while, fell back asleep.

⊷≋⊷

Every morning for the next sixteen days, Hunt awoke shaking and covered in sweat from the same dream at exactly the same time. On the nineteenth day after the dreams started, he slept through the morning. He awoke at nine and realized that he hadn't had the dream for the first time in a long time. He got dressed and went into the family room.

"Morning, Scotty. "How did you sleep?"

Scott rubbed his eyes and looked at his dad. "Not well. There's something I need to tell you."

"I have something I need to talk with you about, too. We may have a serious problem.

Oh, rats, there's the dang phone."

Hunt was not one to use even the mildest profanity, regardless of the situation. He was always in control. No one had heard him say so much as a damn or hell in the past twenty years, regardless of the intensity of the situation.

"I'll get it, Pop." Scott reached for the disruptive device. "Hello."

"Your journey must begin in two days at Lupton," the reedy, metallic voice began as soon as Scott answered the phone. "You are in mortal danger," it hissed. "You will meet a stranger in Lupton. You must take him with you on your journey if you want to find the technology and live," it warned growing louder and louder. "Two days." Then, silence.

Scott put the phone down and turned to his dad, "I didn't hear the first phone call you got about the journey but I would bet the guy on the other end of this call was the same guy who made that first call." He repeated the message to his dad.

"Our caller certainly is making it more difficult to refuse his invitation."

"That's for sure. By the way, what did you want to talk to me about, Pop?"

"What? Oh...oh yeah. Sit down. I've had a number of strange dreams over the past couple of weeks that all ended precisely at 2:20 each morning and each was almost a duplicate of all the others except that the dreams ended with—"

"With different words?" Scott interrupted.

"Yeah." Hunt studied his son. "Eighteen different words to be exact. How do you know that?"

"I'll be right back." Scott headed towards his bedroom.

Hunter watched his son's retreating back. *How could he know about the words?*

Scott returned carrying a piece of white paper. "Were these the words at the end of each of your dreams? Journey, LEAX, 66, territory, razed, explosion, cave, zoo, tube, hades, antre, gunfight, A-bomb, numbers, oatie, goldfish, and –he took a deep breath–death and Scott." Hunter could tell Scott was having a problem with the fact of the last two words.

"Yes, all the same words in the exact order. What is going on?"

"I had a dream that had all these words in it but I don't know why, Dad. When I woke up, it was like I could hear the words over and over again until I wrote them down."

"I think they might have a connection to the phone calls and the journey the caller keeps talking about. But, what bothers me is how the caller got into our minds, implanted the same words and images, and then controlled both our dreams." Hunter noticed Scott still had the troubled look on his face. "I'm concerned too, Scott, about why your name is on the list right after the word death?" There was a moment of silence and then Hunter concluded, "Perhaps, someone's just given us our final answer to the question of whether we should accept the caller's invitation to go on the journey."

"There's a chance this could be a prank and that we will look foolish if we go," Scott told his dad. "But, having my name on the list with the word death also gives me the creeps. What if we didn't do anything and this is real?"

"I agree with you, Scott.' He reached out and grasped his son's shoulder. "We simply can't afford to ignore this."

After a moment of pregnant silence, Hunt declared, "We're agreed then. We're going on the journey."

Reluctantly, Scott nodded his head. Hunt went out into the kitchen where Margie was fixing dinner.

"Hi, sweetheart, you look a little lost. Did something happen?"

"I have to tell you something and I'm having a hard time with it." Margie put down the mixing spoon and came over to Hunter.

"What is it?"

"You'd better sit down," Hunt suggested. Margie sat down without taking her eyes off him.

"Do you remember about three weeks ago, I kept waking up at 2:20 every morning sweating from the same bad dream?"

Margie shook her head.

"It happened eighteen times with different words. Scott had a dream last night and heard and saw the same eighteen words in the same sequence I did. Exactly the same words in the same order. All that in addition to another phone call that told us to prepare for a journey and that our lives depended on our taking that journey."

"I don't understand what that means. How could a journey that you aren't going to take cause your death?"

Hunter's expression changed as he prepared to tell his wife about their decision.

"We have to go to be sure for all of us."

"Please tell me this is a joke and that you aren't going to risk your lives on this . . . this idiotic journey idea based on an unfounded feeling and voice from nowhere? You can't be that naïve." She was never one to mince words.

"No, this isn't a joke. We have to go. Scott had the option of staying behind but he chose to come along with me. With two of us, I'm sure everything will be fine."

"But, what if it isn't? You do remember what happened the last time you had a premonition about something? Scotty nearly died over something absolutely stupid."

Hunter tried not to remember the anguish that Margie and he went through. It was the only time in their entire marriage that they had dealt with so much anger and finger pointing that they were only days away from a painful split-up.

"I wish you would have talked to me before you made the decision. I am part of this family, too."

"Yes, you are an important part of this family," Hunter responded in a regret-filled voice. "But I don't know what to expect. I'll need you back here for support but I promise I'll keep you informed as we go along."

"I am not happy with you right now, Dr. Johnson," Margie's voice was uneven. "You need to keep remembering that. I know you're looking out for our best interests, like usual. So just let me say this. If you don't call me every night and let me know that Scott and you are all right, I will hunt you down and make your life miserable." Hunt knew she was joking but, at the same time, he didn't want to find out how much of her comment was a joke and how much was a guarantee.

Margie continued to glare at him and Hunter felt it. But she also came over, softly touched his face, and looked warmly into his eyes.

"Do what you have to do, sweetheart. You aren't out of my doghouse yet and you won't be for a long time but I still love you." Slowly, he stood, hugged her, and then walked into the living room.

"How'd it go, Dad?"

"She was angry, but concerned about us as mom always is. I can't blame her though. If you listen to that story without knowing what we know, we...I...sound like a wild man. I guess there is nothing left for us now but to get ready for our trip." Scott and Hunter walked out to the garage where the camping gear was stored to begin packing Hunt's SUV. Everything fifteen years of camping had taught them to have ready, they had ready to go including the food supply.

"Do we know how long we're going to be gone, Dad?"

"No."

"Do we know where we'll be going?"

"No."

"Will we need to camp out?"

"Don't know."

"Will we need extra food?"

"Maybe."

"How many people will be with us?"

"Haven't a clue."

"So, basically, we're off on another 'well-planned' Hunter Johnson adventure?"

"Sounds like it, doesn't it?" Hunt smiled. They finished loading their camping equipment, supplies, and food and then went back in the house to go to bed. Hunt quietly went into the bedroom where Margie lay sound asleep or at least it appeared that way.

"I hope we're doing the right thing," Hunter spoke softly. Margie opened her eyes and stared at the wall. He undressed, lay down, and, after about thirty minutes of tossing and turning, drifted off to sleep. Margie was not that lucky.

The Journey Begins

At six, Hunt crawled out of bed and went into the bathroom to dress so he wouldn't wake Margie. When he finished, he went to the garage where Scott was waiting.

"Morning, Dad. Ready to go?"

Hunter stopped as he was getting into the car. "I have to talk to mom one more time." As they walked back into the kitchen, the paper sitting in the middle of the table caught Hunt's eye. He walked over, picked it up, and read, "I love you too much to accept that this might be the last time I see either of you. I hope you find whatever it is you're looking for and that you and Scott come home safely to me. I will be here waiting for you to call me every night. Love you. Doris."

Hunter lowered the note and saw Margie standing in the doorway with her arms crossed. She stepped into the kitchen and kissed Scott on the cheek. "I wrote that because I wasn't sure I could say good-bye in person, Hunter. But, after I thought about it, I realized that I couldn't say good-bye without doing it in person."

"I promise you. Nothing's going to happen to us," Hunt reassured her.

"You and Scotty take care of one another." She hugged Scott and shared a final warm embrace and a kiss with Hunter. He could not miss the tears that were welling in his wife's eyes. The two men headed out the door.

They got into the car and Hunter backed it out into the street. He saw Margie looking out the kitchen window at them. They waved a final good-bye.

Hunt stopped the car abruptly. "Did we bring the words?"

"Have it right here." Scott patted his shirt pocket. Hunt put the car in drive and began the same drive through town he had made a hundred times before. But for some reason, this time it felt like a place he had never been.

When they passed the Big Boy hamburger restaurant at the junction of US 60 and 70, Scott looked at the parking lot. "Boy, did we have some good times here."

"Yeah, I understand you and the basketball team ate four whole cows there one weekend and, when they ran out of hamburger, you got angry and ate the bumper off the manager's car." Hunter chuckled and Scott just shook his head.

Soon, they were leaving the city limits and Hunt increased the speed of the car. "Scott, are you awake?" The response was a loud snore. He debated waking him up to share the beauty of Salt River Canyon but decided not to. The road traced a serpentine footprint down to the river, crossed the picturesque old bridge, and then switchbacked up the canyon's reddish north wall. A series of quick left and right turns jostled Scott from side to side and woke him up. He yawned. "Are we getting near Show Low?"

"About five miles."

"I'm sure glad I wasn't hungry when we left the house. It's only ninety miles to Show Low and driving at … let's see … twenty-two miles an hour should get us there for breakfast … next Friday. Do you need me to show you how to take off the emergency brake, Pop?"

"Why don't you go back to sleep? It was so much nicer in here when you weren't running your pie hole." They drove into Show Low and found a clean, quiet looking restaurant. Hunt navigated the car into the parking lot.

"You gonna come in, Scott, or do you want me to have them run a couple of cows by you so you can pick what you want for breakfast?" Scott mumbled something under his breath. Hunt turned off the ignition, checked everything, and then got out. The two walked up to the door.

"Now, don't scare these folks. They're used to people who order one, maybe two items off the menu, not the entire menu. In fact, do me a favor."

"I know I'm going to regret this but 'now what'?"

"If you're going to order like you do at home, I want them to put me at a different table preferably in a different restaurant."

"Yeah, I'd prefer that too, old man," Scott retorted "Being alone will give you enough time to cut and chew your one pancake. Don't take too long, though. They'll need the table for the dinner crowd in about ten hours." They sat down at the nearest table and picked up the menus.

The atmosphere turned serious. "I hope mom is all right."

"Me too, Scotty. Me too."

The waitress appeared at their table. "Can I take your orders?"

Hunt chuckled to himself. "Coffee, OJ, bacon, two eggs over easy, and one pancake, please."

Then, she turned to Scott. "Can I get a double order of stuffed French toast, five slices of bacon, five sausages, four eggs over easy, chicken fried steak, an extra-large order of hash browns, and a tall glass of milk?" The waitress stopped writing, stared at Scott in disbelief, and then finished the order.

Hunt couldn't resist. "Does that come with a grazing bag and shovel?" The waitress walked away, laughing, as Scott took an imaginary swing at Hunt. The mood at the table changed again.

"Was mom right? Have we lost our minds? You know me, Pop. I like the adventure of not knowing where I'm going, but this feels like a major disaster and we're the guests of honor."

"I agree, son. But the elements of what got us to this point are so disconcerting that I still don't think we had any real choice in the matter." After finishing their breakfast, father and son got up to leave. Hunt left a good tip remembering the look on the waitress's face and that she had to make four trips to bring Scott all his food.

At the car, Hunt put the key in the ignition and turned to Scott. "Now that your stomach is full, I guess you'll be going back to sleep?" There was no reply as Scott was moments from nodding off.

Since Scott is asleep, I think I will give Margie a call. He got out of the car, found a quiet area, and started punching phone keys. The phone rang four times and then Hunter heard a familiar voice. "Hello. You've reached the Johnson's. Would you please leave a message?" Hunt thought about just hanging up but decided against it.

"Margie, I am sorry we left without time to carry this conversation into greater depths but I am truly concerned about this whole episode. If we didn't do anything, there was a possibility that something serious could have happened to both Scott and me. I promise I will keep you informed as the trip progresses. I love you, sweetheart. Bye." Hunt pushed the end button, took a deep breath, and then put the phone in his pocket. He walked back to the car, got in, and started the engine. Scott was snoring softly as Hunt headed the car north.

Lupton

Scott's monotone snoring, a filling breakfast, the peaceful scenery, the lack of traffic, and the hypnotizing sound of tires on pavement were an open invitation for Hunter's mind to wander. He drifted back to that strange day in 1966 in Kecksburg when he got the phone call from Diane Ray, the wife of Chris Ray, the disc jockey at WHJB, who had been the first to report on the crash that evening in 1965.

"This is Mrs. Ray, Hunter. Can you come over but can you do it without anyone seeing you?" She sounded scared to death.

"Sure, I'll be right over."

He knocked on the back door and a voice whispered softly, "Hunter, is that you?"

"Yes, Mrs. Ray, it's me."

"Are you alone?"

"Yes, Mrs. Ray." Then he heard the lock click and the door open slowly.

Mrs. Ray glanced around furtively and whispered, "Come in quickly." They went into the darkened living room and Mrs. Ray pointed to a manila folder on the table. Hunter picked it up.

"After my husband's funeral, I was cleaning out his file cabinet and found this. I remembered you'd been actively involved in trying to find information about the saucer crash and I thought you'd like to see these." Hunter opened the envelope and pulled out two pieces of paper. One was a letter with a Washington, DC address.

A blurry, wrinkled black and white picture that had been enlarged was the other item.

When he saw the picture, he let out a low whistle. "Holy cow." The picture showed a light-colored, bell-shaped object about twelve feet long encircled with a band of strange markings similar to hieroglyphics and also a strange triangular shape with a circle on it. Hunter realized it must have been the crashed UFO that the army swore didn't exist.

Then, he picked up the letter and began to read:

"We're aware that you have a picture of the craft that crashed in Kecksburg in 1965 and that you've been hiding it from your government. We want that picture. Until we come to get it, you're to say nothing about it to anyone and you're not to show it to anyone for any reason under penalty of death."

Hunter frowned when he saw the initials 'SAB' in white on a black square at the bottom of the letter. *Have I seen those initials before?*

"Do you think they are threatening to kill him?"

"Not threatening, Hunt. Did." Her voiced cracked as she continued, "Based on what the coroner found, it appears someone was afraid that Chris was getting ready to tell the world the truth so they poisoned him."

"I suggest that you hide these and contact the police." Hunter turned to leave. "Call me if you hear anything else."

When Hunter left Mrs. Ray's house, he noticed a large black sedan parked across the street.

A deep pothole in the road jarred the steering wheel out of Hunt's hands and interrupted his thoughts. He realized that they were nearing the end of the journey. *Or maybe the beginning*, he thought.

Scott's voice broke the silence. "What do you think those eighteen words have to do with this trip?"

"There has to be some kind of connection among the words but I can't figure it out. Maybe we're trying too hard. Let's consider the sequence of the words. The first word is *journey*."

Scott thought a moment. "Wait, the voice on the phone told us 'prepare for your journey' and then later 'are you ready for your journey'...not trip but journey. Now we have a plausible explanation for journey but the next word is just weird."

"Who or what is a LEAX?"

"I don't know," Scott answered, "but I bet we're probably going to find out shortly. We're less than a mile from Lupton." He paused, "Where do you think we're supposed to meet this stranger?"

"I don't know."

Lupton was not very large and there was only one gas station in town so Hunt drove in and pulled up to the pumps. The review of the words stopped when the car did. He and Scott watched a mangy, brown emaciated dog come out of the station, shake himself, slowly scratch one ear, and then walk up to their vehicle.

"At least someone is happy to see us," Scott joked.

The dog sniffed each one of the tires before deciding to baptize the right rear one. After he finished, he checked out his handiwork, walked slowly back into the station, and found a quiet corner. Meanwhile, Hunter was getting out of the car.

"Remember the phone call, Scott. Watch for any person, however strange, who might be walking toward the car and let me know when you see him...or her."

Scott scanned the immediate area around the station and saw a blue light flash behind a nearby building. He saw a single figure come out from behind that building and begin walking in their direction.

"You mean like that guy there?" Hunt stared at the individual. He estimated the stranger to be about six feet tall. He was wearing a silver blue coverall that appeared to be a lab coat. Visually, he was definitely humanoid.

"Yup, this might be our guy."

Scott focused on the stranger's face as he neared the car. His eyes were closer together and slightly larger than humans. Scott also noticed that the pupil and the iris seemed to be the same color giving the impression of a larger than normal set of eyes. He wore a transparent belt that held two small objects.

"Are you Hunter? I am the one who is to accompany you on your journey."

Hunter nodded and finished filling the gas tank. When he was done, he opened the car door and got in. He sat there waiting for him to take the next step.

It might be better if I got into the backseat so that the stranger would have to sit in the front seat where dad and I both could watch him, Scott thought to himself.

When Scott had moved, the stranger opened the passenger door and sat down. After several uncomfortable moments, the stranger began. "My name is LEAX. I am a time traveling terrestrial."

Strange name, Scott thought.

He didn't say extra-terrestrial. I wonder what that means? Hunter thought.

"Because of conditions that I can't explain to you yet, I would like to wait until we can stop in a more private place to continue this conversation. There's a place called Querino Bridge near here. Can we travel to it now?"

"Will you tell us what this is about first?"

"I cannot for your safety and mine," LEAX responded.

"All right, we'll go there but then you'll have to tell us what is going on, what all those words mean, and why Scott and I are here."

"I will tell you at the bridge."

They drove the next twenty-five miles in silence. Hunt glanced at Scott in the rearview mirror and then at LEAX, who showed absolutely no emotion. Hunt turned on the radio to try to help break the tension but could only get static.

That's strange. This is a satellite radio. It never has static. It's either on or off. He glanced at LEAX. *I wonder if this guy has anything to do with it?*

Hunter turned off the Interstate at the Querino sign, drove the short mile to the bridge, and then stopped the car. The bridge was posted 'no crossing' as the state was getting ready to demolish it.

Another example of the blatant indifference to history that man continues to display. We'll be lucky if any part of 66 is left in fifty years, Hunter said to himself.

"We're here. What's your story?" Hunter saw LEAX reach into his belt and touch one of the objects. A sphere of blue light swirled around the alien and he vanished without a sound.

"What the hell just happened?" Hunter couldn't believe his eyes. He began casting around furiously while trying to control his emotions. His dad's outburst shocked Scott. *Dad's record for not using profanity disappeared just as quickly as LEAX did.*

Within seconds, LEAX materialized in the front seat next to Hunt. He appeared exactly like he did when he left except that now a thin layer of dust covered him.

LEAX saw the strained look on Hunt's face. "I just checked back through time to see if there was anything unusual about the area that might compromise what I am about to tell you. I am sorry I was gone a little longer than I wanted to be."

"A little longer? You were gone less than ten seconds."

"Only to you. In reality, I was gone for half a day."

"All right, what's this all about?"

"As I told you, I am a time traveler sent to assist you on your journey. I am a member of a race of crypto-terrestrials called Oent'rfazr. We're not from outer space but rather we now live and have always lived here on earth."

"What do you mean *always*?" Hunter prodded.

"There never was a time when we didn't exist on earth. We are born here and we die here. We travel here before we're born and after we die."

Hunter understood the basics of time travel because of his research but this was pushing even his extensive envelope of understanding and believability far beyond anything he could grasp.

"We are renowned for the technology we developed that allows us to travel in four dimensions. Unlimited travel opportunities to go anywhere and do anything are available if not impeded by time constraints. But, after a while, even that incredible power wasn't enough for my people. They wanted more and they began uncontrolled experimenting. Some called it reckless. They identified a new approach called corporeal mitosis that would allow the individual to be in two places in two different times simultaneously."

"What does that mean?" Scott queried LEAX.

"A single Oent'rfazr could be in ancient Rome watching Caesar cross the Rubicon and, at the same time, in Globe, Arizona, watching a man named Hunter cross into the future. This activity would have been limited to earth for now but part of the future experimentation would create ways to allow travelers to cross infinite physical distances in addition to temporal distances almost instantaneously."

"How far did they get with their experiments?" The question revealed Hunter's professional curiosity.

"Not far. The constant disengaging, restructuring, and reassembling of the physical, mental, emotional, and psychological pieces of the individual proved highly dangerous and had serious effects that altered, not only the future life of the individuals involved in the study but also their entire species."

The story sounded more like a good plot for a science fiction movie but there was something about the story being told by an actual 'alien' that mesmerized Hunter and Scott and kept them listening and wanting more.

"Did they ever actually split a person?"

"No, but what did happen is that the manipulation of genetic structures produced a mutation called a B'stri. Only a small number of harmless mutations existed in the beginning, but, within several generations, the mutations devolved into an aggressive, dangerous species that did whatever they had to do to gain dominance over the Oent'rfazr. They began to steal the advanced technologies being developed by the Oent'rfazr and adapted them for their own evil purposes."

"What does all this have to do with Scott and me?"

"I'm getting to that. When the Oent'rfazr found out that the B'stri were stealing their technology, they decided to hide it until it was safe to continue experimentation." LEAX looked from Scott to Hunter to gauge how they were accepting all this information before continuing.

"They chose Route 66 to hide the technology because it had played a singular role in the history of Oent'rfazr time travel and because of their familiarity with the environment. However, the B'stri found about the plans and began actively searching here to locate the technology."

"But, I still don't see what this has to do with Scott and me."

"We must now try to find the hidden technology with the clues provided before the B'stri do. But finding it will not be an easy task. It will require the knowledge of time travel, which is me and the knowledge of Route 66, which is you."

"Do I understand that Scott and I have been recruited to help you find this technology?"

"No. Actually, I was recruited to help you find the technology."

Navajo Springs

"Help us find the technology?" Hunter even had a hard time saying the words. He started the car, put it in gear, and slowly pulled onto I-40. As a result of concentrating on LEAX's story and not focusing on the road, they were soon traveling over a hundred and twenty miles an hour.

Scott checked the speedometer and put his hand on his dad's shoulder. "Umm, Dad, I think that . . ." He was interrupted by a siren's wail and the flashing red and blue emergency lights coming up rapidly behind them.

"Damn." Hunt pronounced the word almost defiantly as he realized how fast he was driving. He quickly slowed the car.

Scott chuckled. *It sounds like dad is trying to make up for some more lost time in the swearing department.* Hunter watched the Highway Patrol vehicle accelerate almost out of control going around him.

"Twenty-two miles an hour? Twenty-two miles an hour? I don't want to hear anything more on that subject...ever," Hunter told Scott. Scott laughed as LEAX looked at the two quizzically.

Hunter continued decelerating the car to the legal speed limit and mumbled, "Going double the speed limit and I don't even rate a look from the cops. Talk about the luck of the Irish."

"Yeah, but we don't know what your nationality is, Pop, so you better not push that too much."

"What is this journey you keep talking about, LEAX? What journey and where? What does it have to do with the eighteen words that Scott and I heard during our dreams?"

"The Oent'rfazr traveled through time along Route 66 and planted clues to help us find the technology they hid. Our journey is to travel along 66 and find the indicators that together will help guide us to the technology."

"What indicators are you talking about, LEAX?"

"They are mapRocks hidden by my people."

"What are mapRocks?" Scott looked at LEAX.

"They're part of the high sensitivity, electronic identification network that'll help us find the technology. To find the technology, we must find all of the hidden mapRocks and connect them in sequence."

"How're we going to know where to find them? We don't have a map of where they hid the clues."

Scott spoke up. "Oh yes, we do. Kind of."

Hunter was puzzled for a moment and then his expression changed. "The list."

Scott pulled out the list and began.

"*Journey*. That one is pretty obvious."

"*LEAX*."

Hunter looked at LEAX. "I guess we know what or who a LEAX is now. What's next?"

"*66*. How obvious can this one be."

"It doesn't seem as tough as we thought it was going to be. What's next, Scott?"

"*Territory*."

Hunt thought for a moment. "Maybe I spoke too soon. What could that mean?"

"What do you think about this, Dad? Once we identify each new word, we can then identify the next few towns on the real roadmap that come after the one we just left. Then, maybe, we can connect the dream words with physical places like a weird kind of roadmap."

"Makes sense in a strange way," Hunt remarked.

"I don't see anything connected with the first three words that makes any sense but we have pretty much identified what those are anyway so I will try *territory* as it relates to Arizona," Scott suggested.

"Try to match it against Arizona places on Route 66 that come after Lupton as you suggested, Scott."

After several minutes on his laptop, Scott announced, "I think I have a link to *territory*. Listen to this. Navajo, located in northeastern Arizona, is a small town on the Navajo reservation. On December 29, 1863, a small wagon train of twenty-five men and women coming west from Chicago stopped at Navajo Springs, a local water source. That evening in the middle of a blinding snow storm with no shelter other than a few tents, John Goodwin and the other men in the party were sworn in as Arizona's first territorial government."

"There's the event that I require," LEAX interjected.

"That's good stuff. Where did it come from, Scott?"

"The information came from a book titled *Arizona 66 Ghost Tracks* by a guy named Doc Lee. Ever heard of him?"

"No," Hunter replied. "Probably a local 66 fanatic, who is retired with nothing significant left to do with his life."

"It contains a recap of all the towns, cities, and wide spots on 66 in Arizona from New Mexico to California. It might provide additional information to help us link locations to words."

Hunter saw a road sign that read: Navajo 1 mile. He turned off and followed the sign. The road was not much more than a dirt path, but it only took a few bone-jarring minutes to reach the town.

"Here we are," Hunter announced. "I see a gas station, a small trading post, a number of run down houses, a fenced area with many rusting car bodies, and a mobile home."

Several Native Americans sat on the ground outside the trading post and silently watched as they drove into town.

Scott reminded everyone, "We need to find Navajo Springs."

LEAX turned and pointed at a very large billboard that read: Navajo Springs Monument ¾ of mile. Hunter turned, smiled at his son, and shook his head.

LEAX looked at the objects in his belt. "This is the site of the first mapRock." Hunt continued to guide the car along a winding and bumpy dirt road that ended in a cleared area. He drove over to a small concrete marker and parked.

"Okay, LEAX, now what?"

LEAX took one of the devices from his belt. "This is a time travel activator that we call a Translator. It has been the source of the success of the Oent'rfaz time travel process since the process was discovered. It's not as powerful or as sophisticated as the technology that we seek, but it very reliable."

"Will it work with us humans?"

"It allows any individual, even a non-Oent'rfazr, to move from one time period to another and back with only minor restrictions. The process is quick and only marginally uncomfortable in the beginning."

"Wait. What do you mean by *marginally uncomfortable*, LEAX?" Hunter's voice revealed some trepidation.

"Each individual reacts differently in the beginning until he acclimates to the travel alignments his body has to make. First time travelers can feel nausea, dizziness, sensory loss, and disorientation during the first few transitions, however, the feelings usually disappear quickly."

"Sensory loss?" Hunt echoed.

"Yes, but only for a short time."

Remembering his first travel experience earlier at the bottom of the Old Dominion mine, Hunt thought, *I think I know exactly what you're talking about.*

"I heard you say it was necessary to find a unique historical event that occurred where you wanted to time travel. Why?"

"Because of certain very complicated abstract mathematical and interdimensional relationships, time travel requires different referent points than those used in your three dimensional world. Scott, abstract time does not recognize chronological dates since they're relative and meaningless without a universally defined origin."

"So, you don't need an actual date to travel? Just an event?"

"Yes, Scott. In our abstract time travel, the atomic bomb could be … and has been … dropped before, after, and even during the time Columbus was discovering America. It's called the Chronology Paradox. It was a travel problem for many years until the Oent'rfaz discovered the Incident Referent, which eliminated the problem by bending time around events."

"You said earlier we're looking for mapRocks. How do they work?" Hunt sounded uncertain.

"MapRocks are 'living' markers used to identify where things might be located. They're made of a crystalline shell that contains a bonding fluid that serves the same function as blood. Each mapRock is grown like a plant for one unique purpose. When it matures, it's sealed in a crystal sphere that is magnetically enhanced to allow an entry and exit connection."

"Wow," Hunter exclaimed. "Inanimate objects could be grown like living things. There'd be no way to run out of resources."

"A mapRock is not an inanimate object," LEAX responded quickly. "It's a living thing. The connecting process not only physically links the two mapRocks but it also allows the two different internal fluids to mix, which then makes the mapRocks more sensitive to the emissions of the item being sought. To help find the mapRocks, a parent Locator device is grown at the same time and programmed to be sensitive to the emissions of the individual mapRock families. There can be as few as two mapRocks or as many as a thousand in a family."

"How do you know when you have all of them?" Scott queried.

"The final mapRock in the sequence is black. Its color comes from the unique bonding fluid needed to catalyze the necessary chemical reaction to hypersensitize the entire chain of mapRocks."

LEAX knelt down while holding the Translator, made several adjustments, and then called to Hunt. "Touch the Translator at the same time I do."

Hunt touched the device when LEAX did. Almost instantly, a blue swirling light surrounded them like a cocoon. Scott watched the two men disappear and then reappear within seconds.

"Did you go back in time?"

"Yes," Hunter answered still shaking off the effects of his first excursion.

"Did you find the mapRock?"

"Yes and no," LEAX replied. "We were looking for the location of the mapRock, not the mapRock itself."

"Did you find it?" Scott wasn't sure if he was asking the right question.

"Yes."

"Well, where is it?"

"That's what we're about to show you."

"You mean it isn't hidden in the past?" Scott continued.

"Yes, it is," LEAX answered. "It's hidden in the past, in the future, and in the here and now."

"Why didn't you just bring it with you from the past?"

"One of the limiting travel conditions is that you can't bring things back from the past so our process is to locate it in the past where the Oent'rfaz hid it, leave it there, and then return to the present to find that same mapRock that exists in your time."

"How do we find it here?" Hunter questioned.

"With the Locator, the other device in my belt. Based on the emissions from the mapRock, the Locator will guide us to the exact physical location of the mapRock. It's very similar to the device used in your past to locate radiation sources. When we were watching the event—"

Hunter interrupted, anxious to share his experience. "When we got there, it was afternoon and there were ten covered wagons in a group. The people seemed to be busy unloading supplies and tents and setting up a large encampment. We hid behind an outcropping of large boulders and watched as they went about completing camp and preparing the evening meal."

"What was it like to be right here a hundred and fifty years ago?" Scott's excitement reflected in his voice.

"It was like nothing I had ever felt before," Hunt answered. "Several men went to a wagon and lifted out a large bathtub and set it near where the campfire would be."

"A bathtub?"

"Yeah. They were going to use it to mix drinks for the inauguration–a mixture of champagne and a fluid contained in a certain Arizona cactus."

"That's amazing."

"At the same time," Hunter continued, "one of the people walked over to a wagon and removed a small wooden box. LEAX suggested that we watch what the person did with the box. He dug a small hole under the wagon, placed the box in it, and then covered it."

"I thought it might contain something significant because the person was trying to hide it," LEAX remarked. "The person, who was burying the box, wouldn't have been aware that the box might be used to hold the mapRock so there must have been something else valuable in it."

"We waited until the group was situated around the campfire and then we went over to where the box was buried and dug it up. We took it over near an outcropping of boulders and re-buried it near a specific boulder with white marks on it. Then, we came back here. It was just incredible," Hunt concluded.

"Let's go see if the box is still there," LEAX suggested. They walked over to the boulders and looked through the rocks. "There it is." LEAX went to the car, grabbed a shovel, and started digging. "There." LEAX pointed as a loud thud emanated from the hole. They pulled the box out of the ground and set it on a nearby table. It had been a very ornate wooden box once but the elements had caused it to deteriorate badly over the last century and a half.

"It shouldn't be too difficult to get this open," Scott surmised. They pried off the lid, looked inside, and found an official looking letter and, underneath it, the mapRock. Hunt picked up the letter and opened it. Although he tried to read the content of the letter, the signature at the bottom drew his focus almost magnetically.

"My God . . . Abraham Lincoln. President Lincoln signed this in 1862. Look at this, Scott."

"And here's the mapRock," LEAX noted as he reached in the box, lifted it out, and handed it to Scott. Scott handed the Lincoln letter to his dad so he could take the mapRock.

"So this is going to guide us to the miracle time travel device." Scott wrapped it in a cloth and put it in his shirt pocket.

"Remember, one and only one specific mapRock will connect interactively with another specific mapRock so having the original is critical. Don't forget that," LEAX reminded everyone.

"Are you saying that if any of the mapRocks aren't the right ones grown for this use or if they aren't in the right sequence, no part of the chain will work?" Hunter tried to make sure he understood.

"Yes, loss of any of the mapRocks, for any reason, will make the chain inoperative and reduce the possibilities of finding the technology to zero."

Scott changed the subject. "What do we do with the Lincoln letter and whatever else might be in the box?"

"Wouldn't this make a great research show-and-tell for one of your History of Arizona classes, Scott? After that, we can donate it to a museum."

"A great idea, Dad."

The three men sat quietly at the table that now held the empty box.

"Is this what time travel is all about, LEAX?"

"I wish I could say it would all be this easy, Hunter, but I know it won't be."

Scott picked up the Lincoln letter again and shook his head in amazement as he re-read it.

"I bet you didn't figure on finding Mr. Lincoln when you got up this morning, Scott."

"I didn't figure on finding him or any other great man when I got up this morning."

LEAX had been listening closely to their conversation. "Who is this Lincoln person?"

Scott watched the transformation in his dad's face that occurred whenever he talked about Lincoln. "He was the right man at the right time. He was the 16th President during the most violent and contentious time in the life of our country."

LEAX was quiet and then began, "One of my early travel assignments was to come to a different part of your country during the event you called the Civil War. Is that what you're referring to?"

"Yes. What did you do? Where did you go?" Scott needed more details.

"I was sent to that time period by our research scholars to see if I could find a document they needed."

"Where did you go, LEAX? Was it by any chance the White House?" Scott's voice barely concealed his excitement.

"Yes, I believe that is where it was. I watched a tall, gangly man with coarse black hair, a black beard, and a wrinkled face dislodge a brick from a fireplace, place a piece of paper in the cavity, and then replace the brick. He then went back and sat down at a large desk and put his head in his hands."

"You saw President Abraham Lincoln in his office . . . alive?"

LEAX just looked at Scott.

"Could I use your device to go back to see President Lincoln myself?"

"Of course," LEAX answered, "whenever you want but first you must get travel approval."

"From who?"

"I will show you when we can travel safely again," LEAX told Scott.

They got into the car and Hunter drove back to the Interstate.

"I have more to tell you," LEAX began. "The chemical experimentation ultimately created the B'stri. Over time, they became the stronger of the two species, which intensified their propensity for violence. The Oent'rfaz were wise enough to see that the B'stri were likely to steal their technology by whatever means possible and then use it to dominate them. Our leaders devised a plan to conceal the various parts of the new process in areas not frequently visited by the B'stri."

"Route 66?"

"Yes, Scott. They chose it because of their familiarity with the region, the relative geological stability of its landscape, and the lack of any significant change in people or structures along its Arizona path. It was also a major choice because of the extensive lava flows that ran under and aside the old highway."

"What does lava have to do with time travel?"

"Lava provides a conductor conduit for the transmuting effects of the travel process, Scott. The lava tubes were ready made paths for time travel."

"We used a lava tube as a conduit when I traveled forward last month," Hunter reminded his son.

"Once the B'stri possessed the technology," LEAX continued, "they could travel in time to change anything that didn't support their goals and beliefs. Imagine that your President Lincoln never existed or that your country lost every war it ever fought."

"Could they really do that?"

"Scott, what would happen if your family left the house one morning, didn't come back, and you found out they never existed? LEAX turned to Hunter. "If you don't want a world without Margie and Scott, you can't fail on our journey."

"I don't know anything about these people and, up until today, I didn't even know they existed. Why did they target me?"

"Something you may do in the future or may have already started has tagged you as an enemy of the B'stri. To prevent you from finishing what you're doing or whatever it is that you will do, the B'stri have determined that you must die. Yours is a clear task and one at which you cannot fail. If you do, you and all that you know and love will never have existed."

The Lost Village

Hunter was quiet as he drove thinking about the B'stri and how they were already reshaping his future.

"Does anybody have an idea for the word 'razed'? What could have been on Route 66 that is no longer there? A building? A car? A sign? A mine? A rock? An animal? A town?"

"Considering man's incredible indifference to the value of anything historical, Scott, almost any of those things could be the answer," Hunter replied.

"How about a town?" Scott repeated slowly. "One of my professors told us that, since Arizona became a territory in 1863, historians estimate that over four hundred different Arizona sites have vanished from the face of the earth."

"How many on 66?"

After a quick check on the laptop, Scott answered, "Seventy-four of those vanished sites existed along Route 66 between New Mexico and California, Dad, and twenty-four of those existed between Flagstaff and the New Mexico border. Canon, Querino, Bibo, Rimmy, Manila, Havre, Moqui, Diablo, Connor, and Arrow are a few of the sites. Any sound familiar?"

"Do we have any kind of information about what those lost sites may have been and, specifically, where they might have been located?"

"Let me see if I can find anything in Doc's book."

"What is the nearest town we haven't passed, Scott?"

"We're about thirty miles from Holbrook, Pop."

Hunt saw an intersection and began to slow the vehicle. He pulled onto a side road and stopped. "Let's wait and see if Scott tells us we have to back track."

"I have some good news and some bad news. I found a string of lost villages that existed between the New Mexico border and Flagstaff."

"And the bad news is?"

"Most locations are best guess estimates about where the site might have been."

"Great." Hunter's frustration was beginning to show.

"Can you guide us to the different locations?" LEAX quizzed Scott.

"I think so," Scott replied. "A lot of the reference points came from information and records that are antiquated and many were partly based on the memory of very old persons. It's possible the points are no longer there or maybe never were. But we shall see."

"LEAX, how close does your device have to be to the mapRocks to work?"

"About a mile and a half, your measurements."

Hunt turned to the front of the car, put both hands on the steering wheel, and then lowered his head.

"This sounds like another typical Johnson adventure. We may or may not be able to find a site that may or may not have existed with a device that may or may not work in an area that may or may not be the correct location. You can't say it won't be interesting."

"And finding the sites will take more luck than a convention of your leprechaun brothers carrying bushels of four leaf clovers," Scott concluded.

Hunter took a deep breath. "Scott, where should we be going?"

"The first four sites were located before Navajo. I figure we can disregard them since the dream word *razed* is after the one for Navajo Springs and there are bits and pieces of the sites still remaining. So, technically, they haven't disappeared."

"I agree," LEAX added in an unconventional outburst for him.

Scott began reading. "Manila was a small railroad stop that existed close to MP85 near a small singular rock formation north of the highway that resembled extended fingers on a hand."

"What was the last milepost we passed, Hunt?"

"It was MP76, LEAX."

Hunter turned the car around and began driving east back along the Interstate.

"Look, there's MP85," LEAX pointed out.

"According to my best estimate, Manila should be right over there." Scott pointed north to a flat area that had an excessive growth of sagebrush, scattered boulders, cactus, and an outcropping of black lava. They parked the car, pulled out canteens and shovels, and started walking. Several dangerous looking, desert dwelling animals scurried to get out of their way.

LEAX saw an oversized, hairy, eight-legged tarantula scamper into a crevice. "Are there a lot of those things in the desert?"

"Yes and worse. We may see some snakes, centipedes, and Gila Monsters out here today." Scott waited for a reaction.

LEAX stopped dead in his tracks. "A monster? How big?"

"It's just a name. It's only about thirty inches long but its bite is poisonous and once they clamp down, you almost have to kill them to make them let go."

Hunter thought he saw LEAX cringe.

When they arrived at the outcropping, LEAX pulled out the Locator, activated it, and scanned the area. He picked up a strong signal.

"Something is definitely out there." He walked in the direction the device was pointing. The signal faded as he moved away from the two men. He stopped and turned around until the Locator began to register again.

LEAX looked toward Hunter and Scott. "What did you do with the first mapRock we found, Scott?" Scott thought for a moment and then sheepishly reached into his shirt pocket and pulled it out.

"Scott, please find a spot and remain there while I finish scanning the area."

Scott sat on a large boulder, opened his canteen, and took a long swallow. He looked around the area and then noticed a wide crack between two large boulders. There was another boulder in the crevice that resembled a hand with a number of extensions that looked like fingers.

"I think we found Manila," he shouted. Hunt walked over to look. As they stood there, they watched LEAX start walking, stop, change direction, and then start walking again. After several minutes of that, he was still walking in circles.

"I don't think the mapRock is here," LEAX concluded.

"So, what do we do now? Is there anything else we can do to be sure?"

"Not without an event to cross link to in the past, Hunter."

"I couldn't find anything unique about Manila in Doc's write-up," Scott pronounced before the question could be posed. The three of them sat in the shade of the outcropping. The fiery desert sun had drained them almost to the point of exhaustion.

"Let's go to the next site and start over. If we don't find anything there, we can always come back here and try again," Hunter suggested. Dejectedly, they walked back to the car wondering if this is what they would experience at other sites on their journey. They sat down in the car

LEAX put his hand out and looked expectantly at Scott. At first, he wasn't sure what LEAX wanted and then a grin crossed his face. He took the mapRock out of his shirt pocket and handed it to LEAX.

Scott opened the laptop. "The next site was Havre, a small native village where a powerful leader lived who attacked villages in the area and turned the people into slaves. Approximately a year later, the leader was killed in a massive uprising and his village was burned to the ground."

"Wow, talk about bad tenant-landlord relations," Hunt commented.

"Nothing in the village was left standing. After several severe winters and summers, even the charred remains disintegrated and were scattered in the desert. It's believed that the village was located about twelve miles east of Winslow and about three miles west of Manila. Unlike Manila, Havre was allegedly located near an abundant source of water."

"What are the chances that the evidence of the water is still there?" Hunt wondered. "Not the water but maybe the footprint of where the water was, kind of like a dried up lake bed?"

Scott calculated where Havre was likely to have been located. Hunt drove as close to the location as he could get and the three of them got out of the car. They took the shovels and the canteens and walked to the spot that Scott had identified.

"Do you see anything that looks like an old seep?" Hunter commented as he scanned the horizon.

"Yeah, over there," Scott pointed. They started walking towards the lighter colored area.

LEAX activated the Locator and almost immediately, it started blinking. Hunt looked around and saw that it was pointed at a broad expanse of flat, featureless plain.

"It could be anywhere out there and there's a lot of 'out there' out there," Scott quipped trying not to turn his comment into a tongue twister.

LEAX was staring at the Locator.

"What's wrong?" Hunt said.

"I'm getting a strange reading."

"What do you mean?"

"If I point the Locator east, I get an increasingly strong signal like the mapRock is in that direction. But, if I change direction slowly, the strength of the signal dies down to almost nothing and then, as the Locator is pointed west, the strength of the signal increases significantly again. It would seem there might be two mapRocks here instead of just one."

"Not my fault this time." Scott lifted both hands, palms out level with his head before anyone could say anything.

"That doesn't make any sense. Why would they leave two mapRocks in the same place? Could the device be malfunctioning?"

"I don't think so, Hunter. We're going to have to travel back to see if we can isolate each site to see what is happening. Are you ready?"

Hunter took a deep breath and let it all out. "Let's do it, LEAX."

LEAX and Hunter were instantly transported into the past when they touched the Translator. Hunt experienced some dizziness, which disappeared quickly. He looked around for LEAX.

LEAX put his finger to his mouth and pointed. They saw a large group of Native American dressed in brightly colored clothing standing near what looked like a pyre and a large fire pit. They could hear chanting and could see a body lying on top of the pyre.

"Let's get out of sight," LEAX suggested quietly. They hid themselves and continued to watch as the ceremonial activities continued. First, one person talked and then another and then everyone talked and pointed at the body. One person threw dirt on the body. Then two women began to cover the body in colored liquids that looked like paint. Hunter looked around and spotted something familiar.

Hunt nudged LEAX and pointed. "Isn't that the place where one of the readings went wild?"

LEAX nodded so Hunt picked up the shovels and followed him over to the spot. The participants were so intensely involved in the ceremony they didn't notice Hunt and LEAX. Hunt had been digging about ten minutes when his shovel hit something metallic.

"Got something." LEAX came over to the spot and pointed the Locator where the shovel had hit the metal.

"It's not as strong as at Navajo Springs, but there is definitely something there." Hunt knelt down and began removing dirt by hand. He uncovered a small metallic box and handed it to LEAX.

LEAX looked at it. "This is the box that the mapRocks are stored in to protect them for travel after they're programmed. But this one is empty."

"How can that be?"

"Apparently someone removed it after it was hidden," LEAX replied.

"Why did your device react then?"

"It was reacting to the residue left in the box by the mapRock,"

"So, here's another wild goose chase." LEAX looked strangely at Hunt.

Hunter saw the look and immediately regretted his comment. *When will I learn?*

"Why would we be chasing a wild goose?"

"Never mind, LEAX. What about the other reading on the opposite side of the area?" LEAX picked up the Locator and started walking towards the area where the other reading had been the strongest.

"Wait, LEAX, we can't just interrupt that ceremony. They might not appreciate it and start throwing things at us or throwing us at things." Several hours later, they were still watching the ceremony. They placed the body into the hole near the pyre and began another round of dancing and chanting.

"If you point the Locator at the hole and get a strong reaction, can we go back to our time, locate the hole, and then dig it up?"

"I think so, Hunter."

"We have no way of knowing how long this ceremony will last and we need to get back." LEAX agreed and pointed the Locator in the direction of the hole. It registered strongly.

"It's probably in the hole."

"Then, let's get the shovels and get out of here." Hunt and LEAX picked up the shovels and touched the Translator.

"Did you find it?" Scott hit them with the question as soon as they finished materializing.

"We think so." LEAX looked around for reference points but couldn't see any so he pulled out the Locator and activated it. It began registering almost immediately. Hunter and Scott followed him with the shovels.

LEAX studied the Locator for a moment. "We dig here." Scott and his dad dug until they hit something that sounded more like wood than metal. Scott dropped to his knees and started moving the dirt with his hands but he couldn't find any edges. After he had cleared a three feet wide and six feet long section, he finally found the four corners.

"What do we have here?" Hunter sounded puzzled.

"It looks like the top to a coffin," Scott answered. "I wonder who's in it?"

They all got on one end of the board and started picking it up. As the board shifted and cleared the dirt, an angry buzzing sound that most people in Arizona, who hike a lot, have come to fear filled the air. A deadly rattler was announcing to the world that he was ready to take on all comers. The three men dropped the board and jumped out of the way.

"What was that?" LEAX's voice waivered a little.

"That," replied Scott, "was a rattlesnake. It's another one of those desert animals we told you about." LEAX carefully held the Locator above the board and it registered wildly.

"There's certainly no doubt it's under that board."

Hunter stared at LEAX. "I hope you're talking about the mapRock because I don't need a Locator to know there's a snake under there."

"How do we get the mapRock out without disturbing the snake and whatever else might be under there ... including the possibility of more snakes?"

"More snakes?" LEAX's eyes widened in disbelief. They all sat down and began talking about ways to get rid of the snake.

"We could throw dirt on it or stone it," Scott suggested.

"Maybe, if we could provide an easy way for it to escape, it would leave and we wouldn't have to hurt it or endanger ourselves. You know the old saying, they are more afraid of us than we are of them."

Scott looked incredulously at his dad. "If that is true, then that snake is stone paralyzed with fear. I don't know what he figures I am going to do? Bite him first?"

"Let's try providing the escape route first and see what happens. We have to be very careful when we lift up the board. Maybe we can slide it rather than lift it. That will give us the board as a barrier."

The three picked up the shovels, pried them under the board, and lifted up ever so slightly. When the entire board began to move, they heard the ominous sound of rattling again except this time it was in stereo. They continued to slide the board carefully off the top of the hole.

The board was finally off and the guys could see underneath it.

"Look at that," Hunter cringed. Four large, desert brown rattlesnakes had threaded themselves around and through the rib cage of a human skeleton.

Hunter picked up a rock and threw it at the snakes. As he was throwing the rock, LEAX made a sudden move toward him. In a heartbeat, the nearest snake exploded toward LEAX extending itself to its full ten-foot length and opening its mouth revealing two hypodermic-like fangs dripping venom. It buried the fangs in LEAX's ankle.

Hunter managed to yell "LEAX" but not until after the attack was over.

The four snakes slithered out of the hole and into the desert with their rattles buzzing their impending departure. This provided the opportunity to assist LEAX.

"LEAX, sit down quickly," Hunter urged. "Extend your leg and be very still." Hunter carefully rolled up the liquid soaked pant leg so that he could assess the results of the snake's blitzkrieg attack.

"I don't see any puncture wounds; just those two long red streaks," Scott told his dad.

"Get the first aid kit, Scott." Without any major medical supplies, all Hunt could do was wipe away any excess venom, sterilize the abraded area, and make sure LEAX didn't move excessively for a while.

"It looks like when you turned your foot, it changed the angle of the attack. So, instead of a straight in puncture usual in snake attacks, the material in the pants, your shoes and socks, and the angle of your foot caused the snake's fangs to skitter along the surface of the skin as they pumped out venom. That would account for all the moisture on your pant leg."

"Am I going to be all right?"

"Hard to tell right now, LEAX. Some of the venom may have been absorbed into the open surfaces of the abrasions. I took some of the anti-venom that was in the kit and put it all over the abrasions. I hope that will neutralize the toxins in the venom before it's absorbed into the blood stream." As Hunter talked, Scott carefully wrapped LEAX's leg and then helped him stand.

"How do you feel, LEAX?"

"My leg feels a little numb and I feel dizzy as if I am going to fall. Is that a bad sign, Hunter?" Scott held on him as they looked in the bottom of the hole.

Scott pointed at an area near the head of the skeleton. "There's the access hole and would you look at that? There are two baby rattlers nestled in a pile of brightly colored cloth and broken eggshells.

The three men turned their gauze toward the skeleton. The arms were raised in a prayer-like pose but of more interest were the garland of feathers, small bones, and several stones displayed around a crystalline formation. LEAX picked up his Locator and pointed it at the skeleton. It showed a solid band of color.

"Okay, so how do we get the mapRock?" LEAX inquired. Hunt got one of the shovels and used it to lift the necklace away from the skeleton. While LEAX and Scott separated the mapRock from the rest of the necklace, Hunt looked at the contents of the grave.

"We may have found the remnants of the bad guy himself."

They put what was left of the necklace back on the skeleton and slid the piece of wood over the top of the grave being careful not to injure the baby snakes or expose themselves to an attack. Hunt and Scott started covering the wood with the dirt they had removed only a few minutes earlier.

Hunter told the other two. "Look who's back." The snakes had returned but remained at a respectable distance. "Probably checking to make sure their little ones are okay."

They did their best to return the area to its natural condition. As they were finishing, Hunter looked up and saw the sun sinking behind a mountain range leaving a palette of yellow, orange, blue, red, and pink coloring the sky.

"We're done for the day. We should try to find a place to camp tonight and talk about what is waiting for us tomorrow," Hunter told everyone. "We can also redress LEAX's leg and see how it's coming.

Hunter and Scott navigated slowly out of the area allowing LEAX to walk gingerly on his bandaged leg.

Barringer

After the experience with the rattlesnakes at Havre, Hunt was ready to call it a night.

"Where're we going to be guests next, Scott?"

"The next word on the list is *explosion* and the next town is Winslow. It's a small town in northern Arizona situated along I-40. It was established in the late 1800s to serve the railroads and the expansive cattle ranching industry." Scott read a little further. "I think we can rule out Winslow as a possible site. Let's see what is next. Moqui, Leupp Corners, and Dennison. Let me do a quick read." Scott shook his head. "Nothing. The next site is Meteor City. The outstanding sites around Meteor City are the meteor crater and the remains of the old Barringer observatory. The crater is the footprint of a very large meteor that hit the earth some six thousand years ago. It's a mile across, over three miles around the rim, and almost a mile deep."

"Doesn't seem like much of any possibility that the meteor crater is a site," Hunter commented. "What's next?"

"Two Guns. It was a wild place even for Arizona. Lots of stories about the owner of the town, local Indians, and even a zoo full of live –." Scott's last words hung in the air.

"Did you find something?" Hunt inquired of his son.

"Yeah. I found out that we aren't as smart as we think we are."

"Huh?"

"The word after *explosion* is *zoo*. The zoo at Two Guns"

Hunt looked at Scott in the rear view mirror. "That would mean we passed *explosion* already?"

"Yeah"

"But you ruled out all those sites?"

"Let me ask you a question. When a volcano erupts suddenly or a meteor hits the earth going fifteen thousand miles an hour, what is the result?" Scott looked directly at his dad.

LEAX jumped in. "Explosion?"

"Explosion," Scott echoed.

"Amazing." Hunt just shook his head.

"The impossible we do now; the incredibly obvious takes a little longer," Scott declared.

Hunt found the next exit, turned the car around and drove back east. They'd only missed the exit by a couple of miles so the return trip was quick. They pulled off at the turn-off for Meteor City and found a small mom and pop campsite. They checked in and started driving around looking for their site.

"We found a mapRock buried in snakes in a deep hole in the desert. Why can't we find a damn number that is visible from outer space?"

They found it shortly after Hunter's outburst and he backed the car into the site. They got out and went to work setting up camp. Scott and Hunter unloaded the gear and handed various things to LEAX. Set-up went quickly with the almost machine like precision that developed from many years of camping.

Hunter told Scott with mock seriousness, "I believe it's your turn to cook, Scott. Do you remember how you did it last time?" Scott stared at his dad, while waiting for what he knew was coming next.

"All I can say is don't do it that way again. We want food with real taste and everything this time."

"That's what I get for following your teaching," Scott rebutted.

Hunt held up three fingers. "I give it a three...weak, like your coffee."

Scott lofted a potato at his dad. Hunt and LEAX sat down in the camp chairs near the cooking fire. Scott handed his dad and LEAX cups of freshly brewed coffee.

"Thanks, Scott." Hunter took a big sip of the brew.

"What is this?" LEAX looked at the brown liquid in the cup.

"This is a favorite camp drink called coffee," Scott replied. LEAX took a sip and got quiet.

"What do you think, LEAX?"

"I think I like it," LEAX answered. Scott flashed a 'neener-neener' expression at his dad and put the hamburger patties on the grill.

LEAX then commented, "Those smell really good."

"Wait until you taste them," Scott beamed.

"Yeah, and then we will give you something to kill that taste," Hunter warned.

LEAX looked questioningly at Hunt and then at Scott.

"I do not understand."

"What don't you understand, LEAX?" Hunter tried to keep a straight face.

"Your words to each other seem to be negative yet you do not get mad?"

"Do you have a way to tell another Oent'rfazr that you enjoy working with them or you appreciate what they've done?" Scott asked.

LEAX thought for a moment. "Yes. We put our right hand palm up on top of our left hand as we're talking with them."

"Interesting," Scott laughed. "Here we insult one another in a playful way. It's our way of telling the other person that we appreciate them." The popping and sizzling of the burgers on the hot griddle invaded the quiet of the campsite.

Hunt took a swallow of his coffee. "We probably should talk about what we're going to do tomorrow. However, before we do, let's look at your leg, LEAX. How does it feel?"

"The leg does not hurt anymore but it's still numb."

'That is because a little venom was probably absorbed into your body. That is what snake venom does. It creates numbness in the victim's extremities so that it can't move quickly or go very far.

That makes it easy for the snake to catch its victim and to bite it again which causes complete paralysis. The snake can then leisurely swallow and digest its meal." Hunter unwrapped the leg, cleaned the abrasion, and then rewrapped it.

"Then, I have but one concern. We must be ready for any unknown happening tomorrow," LEAX told the others.

Hunt responded, "Yeah, we must be careful of dangerous animals and ground that might collapse."

LEAX looked at Hunter, "and other things."

There's that look again, Hunter thought.

"Burgers are ready," Scott called out.

Hunt handed a plate to Scott. He flipped a couple of burgers on it and handed it back.

"LEAX, this part of the camping process might be a bit different than anything you have seen before so, when you get your burger from Scott, come join me at the table." Scott put a patty on a plate for LEAX and handed it to him. LEAX took the plate and walked over to Hunter.

"When you prepare your burger, you can add many different things to produce different tastes."

"Don't you like the way it tastes now?"

Hunter started to respond but stopped. "Just watch me." LEAX saw Hunt put flat green things, white circles, orange squares, and red and yellow fluids on his burger. He copied Hunt's choices and, after taking several bites, he removed everything but the colored fluids and the burger. He finished it quickly.

"That was very tasty."

"Thank you," Scott replied.

Scott and LEAX sat quietly while Hunt cleaned the dishes and straightened the campsite.

"LEAX, did the Oent'rfazr travel this area a lot. Do they still travel it and might we meet one?" Hunter spoke the question in a louder than normal voice to make up for the being on the other side of the camp.

"No, there has been no approved travel here since the accident."

"The accident?"

"In our history, and some say in our mythology, two time travelers were conducting experiments with the new technology when their travel paths overlapped. There was a major explosion at the point of incursion, which was unexpected. It destroyed all life around it for many miles including those of the two travelers."

Scott stirred the embers with a stick and gazed into the heart of the fire. The snapping and popping of the embers in the campfire along with the airborne sparks contrasted the dark silence of the night.

"I am ready to hit the sack. But, before I do, Pop, shouldn't you call mom?"

"Yeah, I should. I'll do it right now." Hunter picked up the phone and entered Margie's number. The phone rang three times.

"Hello,' Margie answered.

"Hi, Sweetheart."

"Is that you, Hunter?"

"Yes, ma'am."

"I have been so worried. I must have called your phone a dozen times since you and Scott left."

"The phone hasn't rung since we left home."

"Are you and Scotty all right?"

"We're fine and the mysterious guy that we were to meet is a pretty regular guy but a little strange . . . like most of us. It almost feels like he's a part of our family or I am part of his. I can't explain it."

"Where are you?"

"We're at the Meteor Crater."

"What're you doing there?"

"We're looking for mapRocks."

"Map what?"

"Long story, but they're the reason for our whole journey. I will give you all the details later. We're fine and in no danger. We love you and wish we could share this with you now but, rest assured, you'll be the first to hear about it when we get back."

"Call me tomorrow, please, Hunt?"

"I will. I think Scott will have some interesting stories to share with his mom. Good night, Margie. I love you."

"I love you too, Hunter. Have fun storming the castle. Give Scotty a big kiss for me."

"Oh no. You really don't expect me to do that, do you? If I did, then he might think I like him and I can't have that on my conscience. What would my friends think?"

"Oh, you two are just impossible," Margie feigned exasperation. "Good night."

"Night," Hunter replied as he put the phone down. He turned out the camp lanterns and went over to Scott's tent.

"Scotty? Are you awake?"

"Yeah, Dad. How's mom?"

"She said to tell you that she doesn't have a son named Scott. She painted your room pink and orange and she doesn't even like you."

"Aw, go to sleep and give the rest of us a break from your yapping."

"Yeah, she's doing fine but she misses you and sends you a hug and kiss." Hunter walked to his tent, crawled into his bag, and lay there thinking about what had happened today. He felt the beginning of another headache.

———————◆———————

Hunt was up before dawn fixing coffee for the group.

"Everybody up. We're burning daylight," he yelled.

"Hey, John Wayne. Back it up." Scotty's voice spilled out of his tent.

Shortly afterwards, both LEAX and Scott came out of their tents.

"Are you ready to go cratering?" Hunt posed the question.

Everyone drank their coffee quietly while trying to mentally prepare for what was ahead. Hunt finished cleaning the campsite and loaded the car. They got in and got ready for the short ride to the crater.

As they drove to the top of the three thousand foot crest, Scott broke the silence. "The depth of the crater left by the explosion of the first atomic bomb at Trinity was only six feet compared to almost three thousand here. Also, there was no substantial rim at Trinity."

"Uh oh, here we go," Hunter remarked.

"The force of the impact killed every plant, animal, and human within a hundred mile mile radius of the impact site. Winslow, Holbrook, Show Low, Payson, Flagstaff, Camp Verde, Sedona, and Tuba City would have been leveled and over a hundred fifty thousand people would be killed if it had happened today. What does that tell you about the power of the explosion that happened here?"

They parked at the base of the main building and went into the museum. They found a table near a window that overlooked the crater. It was an impressive view. The crater floor was as unbroken as a Kansas plain except for a small wooden building at the very center.

"Do you know what that is at the bottom of the crater? Scott continued his information barrage. "During the mid-twentieth century, scientists tried to prove that the crater was indeed caused by a meteor but they couldn't find any pieces of meteorites. They believed that most of the fragments were buried underneath the meteorite when it exploded on impact so they started digging tunnels to see if they could find any fragments. After many years of searching, the operation didn't locate any significant deposits of iron so the meteorite theory fell into disfavor."

"Do you have the Locator with you, LEAX?" LEAX nodded and pointed it at the bottom of the crater. It registered the presence of a mapRock.

"It looks like our destination is the bottom of the crater," LEAX replied. "It's apparent that the mapRock must be somewhere on, under, or near it. We will have to figure out which when we get to the bottom."

"I'm going to go find out how we get to the bottom," Hunter told the other two.

Scott and LEAX walked around looking over display of crystals and minerals that had been found during the mining efforts while they waited for Hunter.

"Look at that crystal in the upper right corner of the tray, LEAX. Does it look like a mapRock to you?"

"It bears a resemblance to one." LEAX looked at the crystal and read the note under it. "Found at the deepest point of the mining tunnels. This crystal, which is the only one of its kind ever found, has not been identified. Let's see what kind of reaction it causes in the Locator." The device remained dark even though LEAX moved it around the crystal a number of times.

"Does that mean it's not a mapRock?"

"No, Scott. Remember each Locator is sensitized only to one set of mapRocks. This could be a mapRock from another journey or another time. If it is, it means that the Oent'rfazr were indeed active in this area at one time. Perhaps, it's evidence that the crater was indeed the result of two Oent'rfazr crossing paths at the same time. The old story might not be a myth after all."

Hunt saw them and walked over. "Looks like we're going to do some more walking. Remember, the hardest part of this trip will be when we're the most tired so do your best to conserve your energy."

"Okay," LEAX replied.

"What were you guys looking at?"

"We may have found a mapRock in this exhibit," Scott replied.

"The one that we thought was going to be at the bottom of the crater?"

"No, but if this is a mapRock, it's from another journey at another time," LEAX repeated.

"Another time?"

"It would prove that other Oent'rfazr used this area for travel in the past and also that Oent'rfazr may have caused the explosion that created the crater as the mythology suggests."

"Really?"

"Why would I lie to you?" LEAX looked puzzled.

"No, LEAX, that is just . . . never mind."

LEAX looked at the registration book. "It appears I cannot go into the crater. I do not have a last name to write here."

Scott assured him, "We adopted you last night at the campsite while you were asleep. Now you have the same last name as mine, which makes us brothers. Hi brother."

LEAX looked puzzled. "I was adopted?"

Hunter just shook his head. They picked up their flashlights, filled the canteens, and then headed to the trailhead. It took about ninety minutes to reach the bottom of the crater. When they reached the floor, they all stopped, looked around, and then looked up at the rim.

Wow, that is a long way up. I don't know if I am going to be able to make it back out without seriously injuring myself and any kids I might have in the future, Scott chuckled to himself.

They started walking toward the wooden building at the center of the crater. Inside, they found a wooden frame on the ground that had a metal cover. Hunter picked up the cover and exposed a wooden ladder attached to the side of a dark shaft.

"Looks like this is our stairway to the stars." Then Hunter saw LEAX's face. *Tell me why I keep doing this repeatedly. I have to learn sometime.* "Get your flashlights out so we can see where we're going." They removed their flashlights, cinched up their canteen belts, and climbed down the ladder. The first level was ankle deep in Burger King and McDonald bags and wrappers, graffiti signs, used diapers, and toilet paper.

"Talk about a mess," Scott commented.

Hunter looked around and thought, *No respect.*

The pattern was the same as they moved downward through seventeen additional levels, although the garbage and painting seemed to lessen the further down they went. When they reached level eighteen, the temperature and humidity had increased so significantly, they could no longer maintain their pace without breathing problems.

"Everybody start drinking more water now that we're down this far. I don't want to have to carry either of you out because you're dehydrated," Hunter cautioned everyone. He found the next ladder and they continued down. They just kept moving feeling more and more physically stressed until they reached the final level. Hunt read the sign attached to the ladder: "400 feet below the crater floor."

"It looks like we made it," Scott managed to comment with difficulty between labored breaths. It had taken them almost an hour to descend the last hundred feet. There were no more ladders, only a narrow natural passageway in the wall that looked just big enough for one very thin person to squeeze through.

"Listen," Hunter whispered. A scraping noise that lasted for about five seconds emanated from the level above them and then stopped.

"What was that?"

"Shhhh," LEAX cautioned. No one moved for several minutes but it remained quiet. Hunt took his canteen and belt off and handed it to LEAX.

"I'm gonna see if I can get though here." He began stuffing his body into the crevice. In several places, the only way to advance was for Hunter to do a kind of modified moonwalk and pull with his fingertips. He inched his way along slowly trying to avoid scraping his face on the wall that was so close he could feel the friction from it on the end of his nose. He had to force himself to regulate his breathing.

"Ya know, it's a good thing that you have a big appetite, Scott."

"Why?" he expected another of his dad's zingers.

"If I eaten another helping of mom's casserole before we left, I wouldn't be able to do this without getting wedged in, permanently."

"Remember that the next time we sit down to dinner and you start picking on my eating."

At one point, Hunt had to scratch his nose, but he couldn't bring his hands to his face because the walls were so close together. *I doubt that there's enough room between my body and the wall to even slide my hand up to my chest.*

He had to change movement tactics because of the continually narrowing space. He turned his left foot so it pointed left and he turned his right foot so it pointed right. Then, without being able to bend his knees very far, he slid the left foot to the left and then pulled the right foot along to meet heel to heel with his left foot. It was extremely slow going because his hips kept cramping. He dropped his chin to try to look down but he banged his forehead head on the opposite wall.

I sure hope the ground is stable around here. One slight tremor could make me a very famous cave painting, Hunter thought.

He managed to move about five feet in ten minutes. He could see ahead that the crevice opened up into a large area that looked like it was possible to stand up in and move around in. Shortly after that, he slid into the open area.

"Scott and LEAX, come on. It's a little tight for about ten feet but then it opens into a small cavern."

The other two men managed to get through the crevice a little more quickly and into the open area. Once there, they took a few moments to catch their breath and then LEAX pulled out the Locator. It reacted strongly. A number of piles of rocks on the floor looked like they had fallen from the ceiling. LEAX pointed the Locator at one rather unique looking pile. It generated a continuous light. He moved several rocks to see if the mapRock was under the pile. One of the rocks he picked up was oddly shaped and not as heavy as it should have been. He turned it over and found the orange and blue Oent'rfazr symbol on the bottom.

"This confirms that the myth is a true story." LEAX handed the symbol to Hunter.

Hunter looked at it strangely. "The thing I found at the crash site that's on my wall at home. It's the same symbol as this. What does it mean?"

"It means that whatever happened here involved Oent'rfazrs in some way." LEAX was moving other rocks around as he spoke. He found a small box under several larger rocks further down in the pile. He pulled out the box, opened it, and found the mapRock.

LEAX watched Hunter putting the symbol rock in his pocket. LEAX lowered his eyes and slowly shook his head. "It needs to stay here. It's a death glyph."

"A what?"

"A death glyph. See the colored mark on the edge? It means that the glyph marks the spot where one or more Oent'rfazr passed into the beyond. It's a way that we mark sites and leave information about what happened and who was involved. It's like a personalized history record."

"So, wherever there's a glyph, there will be information?" Hunter sought verification for his own 'glyph'.

"Yes."

"Are they ever used in places where an Oent'rfazr did not... pass on?"

"Yes. To leave very important information about an Oent'rfazr or an event."

Maybe my symbol at home might have information about the crash and maybe something about me?

"Are you saying that this crater for certain was caused by the explosion and not a meteorite?

"Yes," LEAX affirmed. "The glyph proves the myth is true. This area has been quarantined and is still quarantined to all Oent'rfazr time travel because of this."

"Then why are we here?" Hunt asked.

Before LEAX could respond, they heard the same scraping noise again except now it was closer. LEAX had that look on his face again. They stopped to listen.

Hunt looked at his watch. "We've been down here for well over two hours. We should try to get out of here as soon as possible."

They began to crawl back through the crevice. LEAX insisted on going first this time, then Scott, and then Hunter. It took LEAX a little more time, as he had to push the mapRock through the crevice in front of him. They stopped to catch their breath when they emerged into the bottom level of the mine.

"Where's my canteen?" Hunter saw it, went over, picked it up, and started unscrewing the lid to get a drink.

"Stop," LEAX shouted as Hunt started to take a drink. LEAX quickly moved to where Hunter was and slammed the canteen out of his hand.

"Why did you do that?"

"That is not where I left your canteen when you passed it to me earlier. I put it near the opening."

"Are you sure?"

"Yes. Someone moved it."

Hunter and Scott watched as LEAX carefully picked up the canteen. He sniffed the cap and then finished unscrewing it. He carefully sniffed the water.

"It's been poisoned."

"How could that happen? We're the only people down here."

"I wouldn't be too sure of that." LEAX's voice was unsteady. "We need to get out of here now."

He poured the water out of Hunt's canteen, sealed it, and handed it back to Hunt. "Whatever you do, do not open the canteen under any circumstances. Promise me."

"I promise," Hunt said as he started up the ladder. It was an endurance contest, not unlike running up a steep mountain. Suddenly the levels beneath them caved in. LEAX watched the dust drift upwards as Hunter watched his face. *Accident of age or does he suspect something else?* Hunter wondered. They were able to make it the four hundred vertical feet in about ninety minutes counting needed stops to counter the effects of the dust, temperature, and limited oxygen.

"I can't believe we've only came this far in almost two hours," Scott commented as they opened the door and stepped onto the crater floor.

Hunter had been watching LEAX climb the ladders and the slight limp he showed going into the mine was now pronounced as he climbed out of the mine.

"LEAX, is your leg giving you a problem?"

"Yes, where the snake bit my leg is numb up to my knee and it's starting to shake. I am unable to control it." Hunter walked over next to LEAX to help him with his balance as they started up the crater wall steps.

It took them over three hours to reach the rim because they had to stop to rest LEAX's leg and to catch their wind. When they reached the top, they sat down to rest and catch their breath. Then, they went directly for water . . . lots of water.

"LEAX, how are you feeling?"

"Leg is still numb, but not like before."

"If it doesn't feel better in a day, we will get you to an emergency room in Flagstaff," Hunter promised. They managed to make it back to car and collapse in the seats before their knees and hips gave way. After taking some additional time to relax, Hunter started the car and headed back toward the Interstate. Everyone was quiet after the day of incredibly intense exercise and two very narrow escapes with their lives.

Two Guns

"*Cave*" Scott called out as he began looking for the next clue.

Hunter and LEAX turned and looked at him.

"I thought the next word was *zoo*?" Hunter reminded Scott of what he had called out earlier.

"No, it was just a lucky error on my part. *Zoo* is the word after *cave*. This one is a bit of a mystery as there're no sites between the crater and Flagstaff that have major holes in the ground. In fact, the only site is Two Guns."

"Two Guns?"

"Yeah. Two Guns was founded as Canyon Lodge Trading Post in the early 1900s. When the road through the area was renamed Route 66, the area began to grow to serve travelers. It was re-named after a colorful hermit named Two Gun Miller who allegedly lived in a cave near the present site. Miller bought some property and built a gas station, a store, and 'created' a number of public offerings that would cause tourists to stop there."

"Public offerings? Is that the new term for tourist trap?" Hunter asked cynically.

"Miller had a number of ongoing problems with community members including shootings and eventually sold out and moved to eastern Arizona leaving his wild animal zoo, the Apache Death Cave, and series of Indian ruins that he had built in the side of the nearby canyon. Miller had done such a good job on the phony ruins that it's still difficult today to tell which are real and which are phony."

Scott continued to scroll down the Internet page and stopped suddenly. He found a picture of the town in the 1930s that included the service station and the wild animal zoo. Across the top of doorway was the word Zoo. He remembered that zoo was also on the word list so he decided to check the list once more to be sure he hadn't again somehow reversed the sequence of the words.

"*Explosion. Cave. Zoo.* Nope, I had it right. We should be looking for a cave."

"Did I hear you say something about an Apache Death Cave earlier?" Hunter remembered.

"That might be it. Good catch, Dad."

Hunter saw the sign for Two Guns and pulled the car off the road into what must have been a parking lot. It was covered with Private Property and No Trespassing signs. Hunt chose to ignore them. They got out and started looking for any unique buildings or signs.

"There are the ruins of the zoo, a small building with the letters RMG on it, and a sign that points to the Diablo Canyon Bridge," Scott pointed out. They walked towards the bridge past an outcropping of rocks than showed black carbon residue from past fires.

"Nothing here," Hunter announced. As they walked back towards the service station ruins, they saw LEAX holding the Locator up to one of the buildings. Hunt and Scott joined him and started checking the building out. Scott found a plate in the corner that showed a dedication date of April 23, 1929.

"LEAX, I found a reference date."

"Okay, now that we have a referent, I suggest that we start our time search at the zoo building in the past. From there we can check for a cave."

"Sounds like a plan," Hunter and Scott agreed.

Hunter and LEAX were preparing to leave when Scott stopped everyone. "You both have done this a number of times. I'm a team member, too, so I would like my shot at going back to the past."

"I think he deserves his chance," his dad agreed.

"I agree with your dad but not at this time. There's still a serious danger involving his life that requires me to keep a constant watch on him. However, I promise you will go, *soon*."

Hunter and LEAX touched the Translator and the now familiar blue swirl engulfed and dissolved them. They materialized behind a group of tourists standing outside the zoo building. Hunter saw LEAX moving away so he looped around the crowd and made his way to where LEAX was.

"Let's see if we can find the cave." They began to walk away from the crowds past a homemade sign that read Apache Death Cave this way.

They followed the path for a distance.

"There are the bridge and the pile of boulders," Hunter pointed out.

LEAX pointed the Locator in the direction of the boulders. "I think we found it." They walked over to get a better look at the boulders and found a blackened opening that looked like it led into and under the boulders.

"Let's get back to our time so we don't raise any suspicions." Hunter and LEAX touched the Translator. Scott was waiting for them when they materialized.

"Where?" Scott asked.

"The cave is in the boulders."

Hunter motioned Scott to follow them. They walked to the boulders and moved around to the back where they found an opening that was covered by several layers of wire fencing. The Locator emissions seemed to stay constant as they walked around the fence.

"Is it broken?" asked Scott.

"No, it just means that the mapRock is probably down in the bottom of cave somewhere, which creates some challenges."

Hunter looked up. "What do you mean?"

"I don't see any way to get into the cave from here. We can get through the fence but how do we get down into the cave?"

"Did we pack the camping rope, Scott?"

Scott left for several minutes and then returned. "Not long enough for what we need, Pop."

"We better have a closer look at the entrance then." They removed the fencing materials and carefully approached the edge. They couldn't see the bottom.

"Exactly what happened here?" LEAX inquired.

"A group of Apaches had raided the Navajo villages in the area, took supplies, killed many women and children, and took several captives. When the Navajo men found out what happened, they formed a kind of posse to go after the Apaches. Knowing they were being chased, the Apaches took refuge in the cave with their horses figuring that if the Navajo's came down after them, they would be easily killed."

Hunter stopped what he was doing so he could listen to Scott's story.

"However, the Navajo were smart enough not to follow them into the cave. Instead, they gathered dried plants, cloth, and deadwood; set them on fire; and dropped them into the cave. Then they began firing their weapons into the cave from above while continually feeding the fire. They kept it up for over twenty-for hours until there was no return fire."

Hunter started to ask a question and then decided to wait until Scott finished his story.

"After the fire died out and the smoke cleared, the Navajos went into the cave and found 41 dead Apaches or what was left of them scattered among their dead horses like so much butchered meat. The horses had their throats cut as the Apaches had drained their blood to use to try to extinguish the fire."

The men were quiet for several minutes as they thought about what had happened where they were standing.

Hunter broke the silence. "Natural formations like this usually have at least one other opening for water drainage and to allow small creatures to seek shelter or protection. This cave might have one." The three of them spread out and walked around the cave but had no luck finding another opening.

"If there is an opening," Hunter told LEAX and Scott, "it's likely the animals went inside to get out of the sun or to escape larger animals. Perhaps there are some animals in the cave now and, if we throw rocks into the cave, it may spook them out into the open. If we keep a sharp lookout, we might see where the animals are leaving the cave."

LEAX volunteered to throw rocks while Hunter and Scott got into positions where they could see the largest area around the boulders. After about five minutes, Hunter saw several animals come out from under a small pocket of broken rocks. He marked the spot and, after calling the other two, began pulling rocks away from the pocket. He could feel a slight draft, which got stronger as he moved more rocks.

"Scott, get one of our mag lights, go up to the top of the cave, and then flash the light around into the hole." Scott got the flashlight, went up to the opening at the top of the cave, and lay down on the ground.

He clicked the light on and yelled, "Ok, Dad." Then he began playing the flashlight beam back and forth. While Scott was getting set-up, Hunter had continued widening the passage. He squeezed into the passageway as far as he could and then waited to allow his eyes to adjust to the darkness.

"That's it, Scott," Hunter yelled. "I see the light moving." LEAX and Scott came over to where Hunter was as he was backing out of the passage. LEAX activated the Locator. The reaction was immediate.

"I'll go get the shovels," Scott volunteered.

He returned and passed the shovel into Hunter, who had crawled back into the passage. The three of them removed rocks until they cleared the passage into the cave. The three of them crawled into the main chamber and stood upright.

"My God, would you look at this." Hunter commented as he looked around the cave. The walls and floor were blackened from fire. The pockmarks on the floor and sides of the cave offered contrasting white spots where rock chips were torn out by the thousands by ricocheting bullets that exploded through human flesh, bounced off walls, and continued to shatter more bodies. Other than those macabre visual reminders, the cave was empty.

Scott touched the rocks chips slowly, "It must have been a blood bath in here."

LEAX turned on the Locator and moved across different areas of the cave floor until he found where the signal was the strongest.

"It should be right here." There was a large, empty hole in the floor where he pointed. At that moment, a shaft of sunlight penetrated the darkness and illuminated the disappointed faces of the three men.

"Now what?" Hunter asked.

"The likely answer is that the mapRock was discovered and removed by one of the vandals."

"Again? Where is it now?"

"Unknown," LEAX remarked.

"So, what do we do now?" Scott asked. "Does this mean that we're at the end of our journey?"

"Not at the end but certainly without any help finding the remaining mapRocks. We'll be on our own and guessing."

The three sat in silence for several minutes and then Hunter admonished everyone, "We aren't getting anywhere sitting here. Let's go figure out the future." They crawled out through the passageway into the open air and then walked dejectedly back to the car.

"I could use something to eat. I thought I saw a sign for a restaurant down the road," Scott remarked expecting his dad's usual comment but none came.

Hunt turned the car onto the old highway and began the drive west. Several miles down the road, they saw a dilapidated old building that had signs announcing 'Route 66 Specials'.

"Looks like we may be able to get some food here," Scott observed. Hunt pulled the car into parking lot and stopped. It was one of those places that looked like it might have been someone's home at one time but was now covered with layers of faded, peeling paint. They found a small table inside and sat down. A pretty teenage girl brought over menus. Scott noticed the yellowing copies of articles and black and white pictures stapled all over the walls and got up to look at them. He noticed one article that stood out because the paper had not yellowed. It was a recent addition to the wall. Scott was careful to read the entire article. The waitress came back to take their order.

"Burger and coffee."

"Me too," echoed LEAX.

Scott finished reading, came over, and sat down.

"Three burgers, two orders of fries, and a soda." As the waitress finished writing down their order, Scott asked, "Are you from around here?"

"No, I'm not, but my grandfather is. In fact, he used to own Two Guns." Immediately the three men focused on what the waitress was saying.

"Really? Does he know the history about the different things that are on the site?" Scott continued.

"I'll say. He's a walking history book about the whole area."

"Is your grandfather here?" Hunter asked.

"Yes, but he isn't in too good a shape."

"Do you think he'd talk to us...about Two Guns?"

The waitress looked at him and smiled. "He'd talk to a rock about Two Guns. In fact he has on occasion."

"May we talk to him, now?"

"He's the back. I'll go get him." She returned with a hunched over old man with an extensive crop of wrinkles and brown leathery skin that testified to his life in the outdoors. He walked slowly up to the table, his half lidded eyes moving from Hunter to LEAX to Scott.

"Hi. My name is Hunter Johnson. This is LEAX and my son, Scott." After shaking hands, the old man sat down and waited.

"I understand that you know a lot about Two Guns. Is that true?" The old man nodded his head.

"It was my life before they came and stole everything. When I bought the town from Indian, it still had all its spirits." The old man spoke haltingly with some difficulty.

"You knew Indian Miller?" Scott asked.

"Yes, he was my cousin."

"What do you mean they stole everything? Who did?" Hunter asked.

"The thieves of darkness. The evil ones. They destroyed signs and parts of buildings and took what had been left in the cave—burned clothing, scalps, bows, feathers, skeletons, jewelry, bullets, everything but I hid the gray man."

"The gray man? Who is the gray man?" Hunter asked.

"The spirit."

"What spirit?"

"The spirit of the cave warriors."

"Tell me about him."

"When I touch him, he talks to me in spirit language."

"Do you know what he's talking about?' Hunter asked the waitress quietly.

"He found a gray skull hidden in the cave after it was first raided. When you touch it, you can feel a light vibration. He thinks the vibration is the skull talking to him."

"Could we see it?"

"I don't know. Grandfather moves it often to different locations so it won't be stolen like the other stuff."

"Will you show us the gray man?" The old man didn't answer. Hunter repeated his question and the old man continued to look blankly at him.

"Do you know where your grandfather hid the gray man the last time?" Hunter asked.

"Yes."

"LEAX, if the skull contained the mapRock and it was in a place for a while and then moved, would the Locator show any residual readings at the site?"

"It should show some reaction but it may be very weak."

"So, if the place the waitress shows us causes a reaction in the Locator, can we assume that the skull holds the mapRock?"

"Or did at one time," LEAX added.

"Would you show us now?" Hunter asked the waitress. They walked out the back door and into an area in the rear of the property cluttered with old signs, rusted auto bodies, parts, and pieces of unidentifiable equipment. They walked until they came to a large metal box covered with rust.

"He buried it underneath the box."

"May we move the box?" Hunter asked.

"Go ahead."

Scott slid the box over to the side revealing dirt that was darker than what was around it.

"This looks like it has been dug into recently." He scooped out enough dirt to leave a hole about the size of a human skull was. LEAX knelt down and checked it with the Locator. It lit dimly.

"Excellent but our biggest problem is still ahead. How do we get him to remember where he hid the skull the last time and then tell us?" Hunter remarked. "Let's go talk to him." Scott could tell his dad was hatching an idea.

Inside Hunter told the old man, "The spirits have a message for the gray man. Can you bring him so we can give him the message?" The old man showed no emotion and didn't move.

"If I give you the message, will you take it to the gray man?"

"Yes," the old man replied.

"Scott, go into the car and get me the small metal container in the glove box and the old camping cell phone from the trunk." Scott looked perplexed but he retrieved both of them. Hunter whispered something and Scott turned his back to the group. When he turned back around, he handed the box to his dad. Hunt gave it to the old man and then nodded his head. The box began to vibrate in the old man's hands.

"Do you hear?" Hunter asked. "The gray man needs to hear the message." The vibrating stopped.

"Spirits, do you have a message for the gray man?" The box began vibrating again.

"See." Hunter said to the old man. Then the vibrations stopped.

Hunter asked loudly. "Do you want the keeper to give the message to the gray man?" The box began vibrating again.

"Did you hear that? The gray man needs the messages." The old man started walking towards the back of the building, watching to make sure they didn't follow him. Scott slipped out the front door and walked quietly around to the back. He watched the old man dig a hole under the Apache Death Cave sign that he recognized from photos taken at Two Guns. The old man picked up the box and listened. The box vibrated again.

My old man is a genius.

The old man pulled a burlap bag out of the hole, untied the cord around it, and removed the skull. He put the box Hunter had given him in with the skull and put them back in the bag. He put them back in the ground and covered them with dirt. He looked around and then moved a small piece of machinery over the hole. Scott noted the location and, when the old man got up to go, Scott ran back to the front of the building and went inside.

"Did they talk?" Hunter asked when he saw the old man. He nodded and then his granddaughter took him back to his room and gave him his medication.

"Okay, let's go," Hunter directed. They followed Scott around to the back. He went directly to the sign and began digging. LEAX pulled out the Locator and it began flashing rapidly and strongly.

"It's in there." Scott grabbed the sack, opened it, took out the cell phone, and handed it to his dad.

"Stroke of genius, Dad. Setting the cell phone to vibrate when I called the number." Hunter smiled and reached for the sack to retrieve the skull. He pulled it out and it indeed was a shade of gray and heavier than he expected. He closed his eyes and touched the skull in several places.

"There's a slight vibration coming from the skull."

"It's probably coming from the mapRock, if it's in the skull," LEAX said. Hunter turned the skull upside down and located the mapRock wedged into the nasal cavity. He pulled it out of the skull and handed it to LEAX.

"It looks like we'll be able to continue using the mapRocks." Hunter held the skull, closed his eyes for a few moments, and then put it back in the sack.

"The skull is still vibrating even without the mapRock."

"Let's clean this up so the old man doesn't suspect that the gray man has been discovered." Scott put the bag back in the ground and covered it up. They walked back into the restaurant and sent a thumbs up sign to the waitress.

Scott looked at the burgers sitting on the table. "I don't care if they are cold; I'm hungry." He grabbed his food and went to the car.

LEAX put the mapRock in his pocket, patted it gently, grabbed his burger, and went to the car with Scott. Hunter paid the tab and told the waitress to keep the change as a thank you for her help in locating the lost mapRock. She watched as Hunter walked out, got into the car, and drove away.

The only sound in the car was the rattling of paper and gurgling of soda.

"By the way, I forgot to tell you something," Scott stopped eating. "Something weird has been happening in Two Guns again."

"Again?"

"When we were waiting in the restaurant, I started looking at all the stuff on the walls. The newspaper article from last month talked about instantaneous flashes of blue light suddenly popping up all over Two Guns at various locations and times. They haven't hurt anybody but, because they appear randomly, no one has been able to get a good look at them. The locals say it's because of the curse of Two Guns.

"We're done here so we don't have to worry about any lights." LEAX turned and opened his mouth as if to say something to Scott but then he stopped and turned back to his burger.

Scott stared at LEAX. *What was that all about?*

Hunt drove out to 66 and headed the car west toward Flagstaff.

Zoo

After leaving Two Guns, the group continued west to Flagstaff along an original section of old 66. Scott was back on the computer looking for descriptions of the next few sites. He alternated between pressing the keys on the keyboard and wiping his grease covered hands on his pants.

"Tsk, tsk, you know what mom would say."

Scott looked at the word list and thought for a second. "The next word is *zoo*. For this one, I don't need Doc's book or even the Internet. The Museum Club in Flagstaff was a key spot on Route 66. The original builder was a taxidermist, who made a living stuffing the creatures he shot on hunting trips. In addition, people in the town gave him the heads of animals they shot after they stripped the carcasses of meat. Over a period of time, the numbers of stuffed animals made it look like a zoo and so it got its nickname."

"Scott worked here during his first year at school," Hunt told LEAX.

"There have definitely been some strange happenings since the club was built, including several resident spirits that make their presence known at various times and in various locations in the building."

Hunter asked Scott, "Having a good knowledge of all the rooms and the strange experiences, where would you be most likely to conceal something like a mapRock?" Before he could answer, Hunt pulled the car into the parking lot and parked under the huge yellow Museum Club guitar sign. The wishbone shaped tree at the entrance was as impressive now as it was when they built the zoo. The anteroom was picturesquely rustic and displayed some of the more unique mounted trophy heads. The bar and dance floor were just beyond the anteroom. To the left of the doorway into the bar was a long flight of stairs that seemed to spiral upwards into nothingness.

Scott pointed up the stairs. "This is where the owner's wife was killed. The police say she fell down the steps but Dean swears that someone or something pushed her or tripped her as she was starting down the steps. She had nothing in her hands and wore regular flat shoes. There were no obstructions on the stairs, and the area was brightly lit." Scott walked the group into the bar and introduced Hunter and LEAX to his former co-workers.

"I am going to show them the upstairs."

The three walked to the front of the club and started up the stairs. Scott showed them all the rooms including a quick trip into the attic. They came back down the steps and went outside to the car.

"It's time to go back and locate the mapRock. Scott, see if you can figure out our next stop while we're gone."

"Great" Scott muttered. "This is my site and I have to sit at home like the little kid." The familiar blue spiraling light flashed momentarily and LEAX and Hunter were gone. They appeared in the museum but now it had a more subdued, almost eerie effect because of the many stuffed animals. The plethora of unblinking eyes created a surreal, almost haunted feeling.

Hunter looked around. "It does look like a zoo. But we need to get busy."

"There aren't any strong indicators here. Let's try upstairs." They went upstairs and when they did, the Locator lights got brighter and faster. They walked through the various rooms and then stopped at the entrance to the attic. Hunt reached for a doorknob to open the door but he couldn't find one.

"What the heck?" Hunter stepped back and looked at the door. He couldn't find a doorknob, a keyhole, or even any hinge marks.

They didn't see any way to open the door or even any evidence that there ever was a door there.

"Now what?" LEAX asked.

Hunt thought for a moment. "Can we return to this site more than once?"

"Yes, but there are serious dangers involved."

"Let's go back to Scott and see if he has any information about the door to the attic."

When LEAX and Hunt appeared, Scott asked, "Did you find the mapRock?" Hunt quickly relayed the story of the non-existent door.

"The original owners believed that the attic was haunted by the spirits that pushed the owner's wife down the steps because she had ventured into the attic," Scott began. "Dean was so distraught that he had the attic door replaced with a solid wall and the door at the bottom of the stairs replaced with a sealed insert that had no keyhole, no doorknob, and no hinges."

"That's a little extreme, don't you think?"

"It became a permanent part of the wall and remained that way for many years. The new owner rather than go to all the expense of reconstructing the walls found that by climbing onto the roof, he could easily get in through the attic window for the few times a year he needed to get in the attic. Several people, who attempted to get into the attic through the window, mysteriously fell and were seriously injured right in front of other people." Hunter stared at the attic window while listening to Scott.

"It doesn't look particularly dangerous."

"One day the owner was on the roof outside the attic window and noticed that a square piece of glass had been cut out of one pane in the window leaving the rest of pane undamaged. The window was boarded and the attic left untouched until the current owners tore down the wall and opened the blocked entrance into the attic. The doors are locked now but can be opened with the passkey. However, the owner keeps the key in a file at home since she and her staff heard sounds of movement coming from the attic late at night recently."

"So, Scott, if we want to get into the attic, are we going to have to use the outside window?"

"Yup."

"Scott, when you worked here, did you ever hear noises coming from the attic?" Hunter asked.

"At first, I thought this was all tourist stuff and the ghost stories were to keep everyone entertained, but, on several occasions, I heard what sounded like furniture sliding across the floor. I even came in early one morning and found the rocking chair near the entrance rocking back and forth with no one in it. I stopped it but it started again by itself. Even stranger, the owners told us that people claim to have driven by the museum well after closing and to have seen a light shining through the attic window.

"What's so strange about that? Hunter asked.

"When they checked the next morning, they found there was no wiring or light fixtures anywhere into or out of the room."

Armed with the new knowledge, Hunt and LEAX grabbed flashlights out of the car, returned to the past, and prepared to climb through the attic window. They stood in front of the building and started looking for the best path to the roof. They found a workable route and soon they were standing just below the attic window. As LEAX was stretching to gain a handhold on the window, he slipped on some lose shingles and lost his balance. He slid down the angled roof and just managed to grab a piece of molding seconds before he would have fallen onto the ground and injured himself.

"Hang on. I'm coming," Hunt yelled. He worked his way down the roof carefully and extended a hand. LEAX grabbed it and Hunt was able to pull him to safety. They both sat down to catch their breath. LEAX extended both hands and put his right hand palm up on top of his left hand. No words passed between them but Hunt somehow knew that LEAX was saying thank you. Together they got up and moved carefully to the attic window.

"Look at the Locator," Hunt said. "It's going crazy." They looked all around the windowsill but couldn't see any way to open the window and the inside sash lock looked like it was firmly latched.

"We need to break the glass so I can reach in and open the lock."

"Wait," LEAX said. He placed his hand at a ninety-degree angle on the glass and then pushed quickly and sharply. The instantaneous pressure created a small rectangular opening just big enough for Hunt to get his arm through without cracking the rest of the pane. Hunter looked at the opening and remembered Scott's story. Then, he reached in and carefully bent his arm so that he could reach the sash lock. He opened the lock and lifted the window.

"I'm going in first. Wait until after I get completely in before you come in." Hunt put both hands on the windowsill and pulled himself up so he could slide his legs into the attic. He was inside in a matter of seconds.

"Okay, LEAX, come in." He moved away from the window to allow LEAX room to swing into the attic. When they were both inside, Hunter said, "Turn your flashlight on so we can see where we're going." The layers of dust all around were mute testimony to the fact that no one had been in the attic for many years–at least no one living.

"Let's find the mapRock and get out of here, just in case we're not alone." Hunter strongly emphasized the last part of his comment. LEAX reached into his belt and pulled out the Locator. The frequency of the flashing didn't change perceptibly as LEAX walked around the attic. As Hunter watched LEAX make a turn, he noticed that, in addition to a number of animal heads, there was a rifle mounted on the wall in one corner.

He started to walk over to the rifle when LEAX called out, "I found it."

Hunter changed direction and walked over to where LEAX was standing.

LEAX pointed the Locator at several discolored floorboards and it glowed continuously. "I think we have what we need." He stood up next to Hunter. Suddenly, there was a scrapping noise from the direction of the rifle.

"What was that?" Hunter said. The two men walked towards the rifle and then stopped suddenly.

"Did you see that movement, LEAX?" LEAX nodded and then pushed Hunter to the floor. The rifle exploded. Hunter felt a stinging sensation in his forearm. Droplets of blood were forming where the bullet grazed his arm. The two lay there waiting to see if anything else was going to happen. When it was quiet again, they got up. Hunter reached for a handkerchief and wrapped it around his arm.

"Look at the floor, LEAX," Hunter exclaimed when they reached the rifle. "Someone has been here since we came into the attic." The dust on the floor around the rifle was scattered in irregular patches leaving bare portions of the wood floor.

LEAX looked worried. "We'd better get back to Scott as quickly as we can." He stood up and removed the Transporter from his belt. Together they touched the Transporter and found themselves standing outside the Museum next to Scott.

"Did you find it? What happened to your arm, Dad?"

"A rifle that was stored in the attic discharged suddenly," Hunter answered. "I guess the powder was very old and there was a misfire. Maybe we created a vibration. It is only a slight scratch. Nothing to be concerned about."

Scott got the first aid kit and dressed Hunter's forearm. *Looks like all those years of first aid training in scouts are paying big dividends on this trip.*

"You were right, Dad. It's not much more than a superficial scratch. It barely broke the surface of the skin."

He put the kit away and then cautioned the two men. "Wait until after the club closes and everyone goes home. That way we will be less likely to be discovered." They all agreed and went back to the car. Scott got in quickly and opened his laptop. Hunt and LEAX opened their doors and sat down slowly.

Scott was quiet for a few minutes and then asked, "What about the gunshot?"

"Yeah, what about that?" Hunter added."

LEAX's chest expanded and then contracted slowly as he let out a quiet sigh.

"My feared situation is becoming real and it's more dangerous than I expected."

"In what way?"

"Do you remember when we camped at the explosion crater?" LEAX asked.

"Yeah?"

"I told you about the B'stri and their role in what is happening now?"

"Yeah?"

"The bullet was his latest attempt."

"Latest attempt?

"Yes, the cave-in and the poisoned water were their first attempt. However, they appear to have determined the best thing for them now is to eliminate you completely so that the current B'stri may not be subject to death at the end of the search."

"So, are you saying that he's trying to kill me as soon as he can?"

"It would appear so and the sooner the better. It has likely become a higher priority than finding the technology but he must do it without being discovered or risk being killed himself."

"What'll it do to the chances for the success of our journey if something does happen to me before we find the technology?" Hunter was not sure he wanted to know the answer to that question.

"The chances for success drop to almost zero. If neither of you are successful, another will be chosen to complete the journey. Someone with your background and abilities."

Hunt's eyes widened. "If neither of us are successful? Are you saying that if I should fail and the B'stri fails, there's a possibility that Scott might be my replacement and that his life will also be on the line?"

LEAX just looked at the two of them.

"Is there any way to anticipate when another attempt might be made?"

"It's logical to believe that each time we stop to hunt for a mapRock an attempt will be made. If the B'stri believes the journey is near the end, he will step up the intensity, number, and level of violence and will not try to remain hidden as he has in the past."

"We have not seen anyone or anything that looks like a version of you along our journey. How can he know exactly where and when we are?" Hunter asked. LEAX looked at Scott in the review mirror. Scott avoided looking at LEAX and shifted uncomfortably for several seconds. Then he was back looking at the laptop.

"What do you think about that, Scott?"

Scott looked up. "What?"

LEAX dropped his eyes. "Never mind, you already told me what I suspected." Hunt looked perplexed. They moved the car to a parking lot next door to the Club so they wouldn't be obvious. It was dark and the three watched the last employee lock the door and leave. Then they got out of the car and walked to the Club.

"We can't all three go inside."

"Yeah, I know, stay here."

Hunt punched Scott's shoulder, gave him a wink, and then walked over to the side of the building with LEAX so they could retrace their steps from last century.

Hunt and LEAX climbed onto the porch and began the somewhat arduous ascent to the attic window again. Meanwhile, Scott had located a position where he could see the attic window and the road but would prevent him from being seen. He looked up and watched in the moonlight as his father and LEAX moved across the roof. *I remember how I felt when I had to go into the attic from the window when Rita forgot her keys. Even in the daylight, it was unsettling.*

The two reached the now unlocked window and crawled back in. Scott glanced warily down the road. No headlights so far. He returned his focus to the window. Hunt pulled a flashlight out of his pocket and switched it on so they could find their way. He noticed the rifle was gone and the attic was cleaned. Lengths of wire lay all over the floor –a sign that workers had been attempting to do something with the electricity.

"Quite a change since last time," LEAX noted. Hunt turned on a second flashlight and set it down to illuminate the area where LEAX would be searching. It only took LEAX a few seconds to remove the floorboards and remove the box. He opened it and saw the mapRock. Just at that moment, Hunter called, "LEAX, come over here."

LEAX put the box down and went over to where Hunter was.

Hunter held up two spent bullet casings. "Do you think these might've come from the rifle that was fired at me?"

"Very possibly."

"But why are there two of them? There was only one bullet fired . . . wasn't there?"

"Maybe something happened after we left." LEAX stopped abruptly and looked around as if looking for something. He stood and walked over to where he had left the box. He knelt down and reached into the box.

"It's gone."

"What's gone?"

"The mapRock. It was in the box when I stood up a second ago and now it's gone."

"Could it have been the B'stri?" Hunter suggested.

"No, we would have seen him and besides he couldn't have moved that fast."

"Try the Locator."

LEAX turned the Locator on and it glowed but the color was less intense that it had been. He began moving around the attic. "Look, it's getting brighter the closer I get to the stairs." The new door locks could be opened from the inside without keys, which made it easy to get down the main floor. The two men walked down the steps and watched as the Locator light intensified.

LEAX saw a faint glow coming from the anteroom. He walked into the room and saw that the light was emanating from one of the display cases. When he approached the case, the Locator light stopped flashing and turned solid. LEAX looked at the display case and saw that the faint light was coming from something in the upper left corner. He looked a second time and then realized what it was. "Hunter, over here. I found the mapRock."

"You did? Where?"

LEAX stepped toward Hunter. "In the display case. Look."

Hunter stepped in front of the case and scanned it. "Where? I don't see anything."

LEAX turned around quickly and looked at the corner.

"It's gone again. How can this keep happening?"

"Are you sure it was there?"

"Yes, I am positive." LEAX shook his head in total disbelief.

"Maybe you should check the Locator again," Hunt suggested.

LEAX looked at the display case and then turned on the Locator. The light was not continuous as before but it was flashing intensely. LEAX stepped into the bar area and the light seemed to increase in intensity. Hunter had gone behind the bar to look around. As he was looking at the rows of liquor bottles along the back wall, he saw a strange object on the shelf.

"LEAX, over here." The light from the locator began to shine continuously. The two men looked at the object.

"It's the mapRock." LEAX sounded a bit uncertain.

Hunter grabbed it. "If this thing wants to go for another walk, it will have to take me with it." He looked at LEAX. "What the hell just happened?"

"I don't know. Things happened here that are physically impossible. The mapRock moved from upstairs in the floor into a locked display case two stories below almost in front of us. Then it moved out of the locked display case– in our presence– to the back bar in another room and there was no one else in the building at the time . . . no one."

"Could it have been the B'stri," Hunt asked again.

"No. I saw no one at any of the places where the mapRock was. You know what did happen though? I didn't give it any thought at the time."

"What?"

"When we were in the attic and I turned to go get the mapRock, I felt an icy cold presence, just for a moment. Then, when I was standing in front of the display case, it felt like I was in a refrigerator. Again, just for a moment."

"Are you sure about that? I was right next to you both times and I didn't feel anything."

Scott saw the light shine through the first floor windows. *I wonder if they are through and have the 'Rock or do they have a problem? Whatever the situation is, hurry up, hurry up.*

Hunter and Scott simultaneously saw a car drive in and park in front of the club.

"We've got to get out of here now," Hunt admonished LEAX. They quickly started back to the attic. Just as they reached the attic window, the first floor lights came on. Scott saw the two men climb quickly out of the attic window.

They're gonna get caught. Scott jumped in the car and drove around until he was underneath the window. The two men dropped to the parking lot, opened the car doors, and jumped in.

"Let's go, Scott." Scott wasn't sure whether to speed off and give the people in the club a clue that someone had been in there or to leave the lights off and drive slowly and quietly so as not to give themselves away. He chose the latter and was able to get away from the club without being noticed.

"Hang on," Scott cautioned everyone. When the car was far enough away from the Club, he ramped the car up to the speed limit and turned west to get out of Flagstaff as quickly as possible. The collective sigh of relief after they passed through the center of town was almost deafening. Scott turned to look at his dad and saw that both he and LEAX had looks of concern as they stared at the mapRock.

"What's wrong?"

Hunter explained what had happened with the mapRock. Scott turned away as he guided the car down the road. *I bet our Club spirits had something to do with that.*

Scott chuckled to himself. *First, adults and aliens. And now, spirits. I can't wait to see what's next.*

An Early Breakfast

Scott drove the car onto the freeway but didn't get very far as the road in both directions was blocked off by emergency personnel and warning signs. He stopped the car and asked, "How long will the road would closed?"

"It's probably going to be about three hours before we get it open again. A pretty bad accident up ahead."

"Three hours? What time is it now?" Hunter asked.

"It's about five thirty," Scott replied.

"I don't know about you two but I don't want to sit around here for three hours twiddling my thumbs," Hunter said.

LEAX looked at his thumbs but Hunt saw it coming and sighed. "It's just an expression, LEAX. I'm hungry. Why don't we get some breakfast and maybe have my arm and LEAX's ankle looked at?"

"Just like living with a goat." This time it was Scott's turn.

Hunt just shook his head. "As if I could hold a candle to your appetite. Okay, smart guy, this is your turf. Find us a restaurant."

"Should we have LEAX's bite checked first?"

"Good point, Scott. LEAX, how do you feel?"

"It's still a little numb but it's lessening and I am not dizzy like I was."

"I don't mean to be personal but how different are our anatomies?"

"There's not much difference on the outside but the inside is . . . quite different based on changes that resulted from years of time travel."

"Are they different enough that a medical person might notice them?"

"Some of them would be very hard to miss."

"I don't think we can risk exposing him now as long as he's improving. If he starts getting worse, then all bets are off and we take the chance."

"Agreed," LEAX concurred.

"Yup, you got my vote, too." Scott turned a corner and pulled into the Mother Road Café, a small restaurant that advertised it had been in business since Route 66 opened. They got out of the car and went inside. There was only one other customer in the restaurant. They sat down and looked at the menus. The waitress came over and took their orders. Hunter laid his menu back on the table.

"LEAX, I have a couple of things that I would like to talk about while we have some quiet time."

"What are they?"

"We know that, if neither the B'stri nor I find the technology, something will happen to both of us. But what will happen after that?" LEAX listened thoughtfully and then stared at the table for a moment.

"Based on all the information we were able to find and load into a simulation computer, the B'stri will continue to get stronger and more violent. They will conquer the Oent'rfazr world and then over take the human race totally subjugating both races. This will occur because the B'stri will have changed history and made it happen to their benefit. Ultimately, all remnants of both races will be eliminated and the B'stri will rule the earth and history unchallenged. Then when they find and use the new technology, they will advance outward into space in their conquest for total power."

"What will happen if … when we're successful?" Hunt asked.

"The next step will be to develop another 'team' to complete the second part of the technology hunt—the instructions on the creation and use of the technology. The computer projects that the second phase will result in both worlds becoming more aware of each other and combining each other's best to implement the new technology. This will result in a new, almost utopian world for both races."

"You keep mentioning computer projections. Why?"

"Even with the ability to travel into the future, we still are not guaranteed that what we project or even actually see will occur. There's still a universal randomness that could change the outcome of a viewed future in some way."

"Wait," Scott said. "Are you saying that all the things you said would happen to my dad or to B'stri are not one hundred percent guaranteed to happen?"

"Yes. There's no known way to predict a future event with one hundred percent certainty, at least not yet. That is another hope for the new technology."

"So, my dad might not die if he doesn't find the technology first?"

"The likelihood that it will happen is 99.99% but, to answer your question, there's still a random chance that something else might happen, possibly worse. However, we don't know what that might be. It might be that he survives or it might be that he is lost during time travel. When you consider the various possibilities..."

At that point, the waitress delivered the food and the three men started eating in total silence. After they finished eating, Hunter asked about LEAX's family.

"Like you, I have a son who is approximately the same age as Scotty. I was told through records that I once had a brother but I don't know anything about him. He was lost in an accident when we were young."

"Do you remember anything about him?" Hunter asked.

"No," LEAX shook his head. "I know very little about my childhood. It has been one of the painful parts of my life."

"Is it possible that the two of you could use the Transporter at a later time to go back and search for information about the missing parts of your life?" Scott suggested.

"We're not allowed to use the Transporter for personal use without permission." It was determined that it would increase the probability of travel accidents and that something might be changed that could affect our race and our world."

"So, you have the means of finding these things out but you can't get permission?"

"No, that's not true." There are many cases where personal travel has been approved but curiosity isn't an approved reason. If we can show a significant need, the request will usually be approved."

"What'll happen to you after we're done with the journey?"

"I'll be given another time travel assignment."

"Do you get time with your family?"

"I don't understand your question."

"When you finish an assignment, do you and your son do things together?"

"At the approved time, we'll travel together."

"What about all the rest of the time? Do you see your family and do things like eating meals together or hiking?" Hunt asked.

"If I don't have an assignment."

"Do your wife and son travel like you?"

"I don't know. They have their own assignments to complete but we don't discuss them."

"What's your son's name?" Scott inquired.

"His name is JONH."

"My name is John, too," Scott said. "My middle name."

Hunter looked at his watch. "It looks like we can get back on the road now." Hunter paid the bill and the three of them went out to the car. Hunt got behind the wheel so that Scott could continue his research on the next locations.

Lava River Caves

"Tube is the next word on the list and Williams is the next town after Flagstaff. Williams is a small town primarily noted as being a railroad center in its early days. Its claim to fame is that it was the location for a type of summit meeting for the Democratic Party with the President of the United States and key senators in 1932. It's the terminus of the Grand Canyon Railroad. Nothing here about tubes."

"Anything unusual between Flagstaff and Williams?" Hunt looked hopeful.

"I remember exploring an old collapsed lava tube with my high school Geology class in this area several years ago," Scott recounted. "Could that be what the word is referring to?"

"Let's go for it." Within ten minutes, they found themselves at the entrance to the lava tube.

LEAX activated the Locator and pointed it toward the opening. It flashed indicating there might be a mapRock somewhere in the area. They got out of the car and went to the entrance. A marker at the entrance titled 'Lava River Caves' showed a drawing of the tube. It showed how the lava at the top of the tube had collapsed because of age and gravity and opened the interior of the tube to exploration. The sign also stated that explorers had gone up to ten miles in either direction without finding the ends of the tubes.

"Oh, great," Scott remarked. "We may get to walk in total darkness for twenty miles looking for any kind of sign and praying that we don't get bitten, fall over a rock, break something, or possibly get lost or hit on the head."

Hunt was getting canteens of water and flashlights to help them along their trip. Together they began their descent into the mouth of the tube. Colored graffiti covered the walls and ceiling and beer cans, food wrappers, bottled water containers, used diapers, toilet paper, and other trash littered the floor.

Just like at the crater, Hunter thought. LEAX stopped and pointed the Locator in both directions. It registered more strongly in the western part of the tube so they turned on their flashlights and began walking that way. The roof of the tube was close to the floor in spots so they had to walk hunched over in places to keep from banging their heads. The condensation of their breath was testimony to their labored efforts to walk in darkness on a very irregular surface.

"It must be a hundred percent humidity down here and at the most fifty degrees," Hunter remarked. They had to go through a side passage where the rock fall had been cleared to avoid the blocked tube. They walked carefully in the quiet blackness for another ten minutes not saying anything trying to keep from tripping and falling.

"I haven't seen anything that looks like a symbol or a mapRock anywhere? Did we go to the wrong place?"

LEAX stopped. "Be quiet and listen." An almost imperceptible rumbling sound began to crescendo.

"It sounds like the tube is collapsing," Hunter concluded.

Crash. Thud. Boom. Crack. Rumble. The confined space in the tube magnified the sounds of rocks and boulders breaking apart, grating across each other, and falling on the floor with such force that the entire tube shook with earthquake like intensity. It began to sound like a war zone around them.

Hunter listened and then realized the sound was increasing in volume and moving toward them at an increasing speed. He yelled, "It's coming our way. Run. Run." The three men had started running when LEAX tripped and fell in the darkness. Scott and Hunt kept running, not realizing that LEAX had fallen. The roof continued to collapse behind them with an ominous, rolling, rumbling sound that threatened to engulf them. Suddenly, Scott realized that LEAX wasn't with them.

"Dad, where's LEAX?" Hunt stopped and looked around but couldn't see a thing. The dust was so thick that there was no way for the guys to know where they were, who they were, or even if someone were standing right in front of them wearing a neon suit. The rumbling slowly decreased in intensity and finally stopped.

"Scotty, stop where you are. Don't move until we get some visibility." Just then a huge slab of the roof fell next to Hunter knocking him down and covering him with dust.

"Are you all right, Scott?"

"Yeah, but I am having a hard time breathing."

"Me too," Hunter replied and then he called out. "LEAX. LEAX. Are you there?"

No response.

After about ten minutes, the air cleared enough to see a beam from the flashlights.

Hunt asked again, "Are you all right?"

"Yeah, Pop, I am fine. I can see you now."

"Walk over to me slowly and let's figure out our next step."

When Scott reached Hunter, they hugged briefly. "We have to see if we can find LEAX. Follow me and stay close in case some more of the roof collapses." They walked about twenty feet and came to a rock fall that had sealed off the tube completely.

"Do you think LEAX is safe?"

"I don't know, Scott."

"LEAX. LEAX. LEAX." They called out his name repeatedly. They stopped and listened but there was no response. After a time with no response, they both sat down.

"It's possible that several hundred or even several thousand feet of tube collapsed and crushed everything on the other side of this plug."

"What if he's dead, Dad? Then, all of this will have been for nothing and…" Scott stopped.

"And?" Hunter asked.

"If we can't complete the journey, it means that…that… you're going to die." Hunt was very quiet as he thought about Scott's words and the strength it took for him to say that out loud.

"We'll just have to find a way to finish this by ourselves."

"But how? We don't have enough information."

"Let's try calling again." There still was no response to any of the hails.

"I guess we better get out of here and figure out what we can do if we have to try to finish the journey without him." They managed to reach the entrance safely and were soon crawling to the surface. Both coughed extensively as they filled their lungs with clean air. Neither said much as they were both lost in their own thoughts. They walked over to the car, opened the doors, and sat down.

"What're we gonna do now, Dad?"

"I think we should find a campsite near here and then see if we can locate LEAX tomorrow. I don't want to leave here without making every possible effort to find him regardless of his condition." They drove to a clearing about a quarter mile from the opening, got out the camping gear and built a campfire ring for the fire. It was mid-afternoon when they finally completed the set-up process.

"It just doesn't feel right without him," Scott remarked. Hunter nodded in agreement.

Hunt and Scott just walked through the rest of their day. In mutual respect, they each gave the other space and silence for reflection.

In early evening, they started preparing dinner. Scott whipped up a batch of his specialty burgers. Father and son sat opposite one another immersed in the deep woods' quiet where only the sounds of the nocturnal animals crying out or walking through the dead ground cover could be heard. The evening breeze immersed the campsite in the relaxing aroma of pine trees.

Scott reflected, "It's been eight hours since the cave-in. I wonder?"

"It doesn't do any good to second guess what might've happened," Hunt said. "We'll just have to wait until tomorrow."

The crackling of the campfire added a new sound to the evening. Hunt started to say something when they heard a noise that sounded like a large animal moving through the dense brush.

"Shhh," Hunt cautioned. They put their plates down slowly and reached for anything that could be used as a weapon to defend themselves.

"Is this when the bears come down out of the mountains?" Scott asked in a quiet voice.

The noise got louder and closer until it was possible to see the bushes near the campfire moving back and forth. Hunt and Scott tensed up. The bushes stopped moving and the camp got very quiet. Scott and Hunter scanned the vegetation around the camp to see if they could see where or what it was. The bushes began moving back and forth again this time more violently. Hunter tightened his grasp on the stick he'd picked up just as a shadowy figure moved out of the bushes into the light of the campfire.

"LEAX," Scott shouted. It was LEAX, much dirtier than he had been that afternoon, but alive.

"Are you hurt?" Hunt inquired.

"I am tired, thirsty, and hungry." They helped him to the campfire and then sat down. Scott got him some water and he took several long swallows and then put the glass down.

Looking at Hunt with his usual non-descript face, LEAX asked, "Is this what it means to be buried in your work?" Hunt and Scott looked at LEAX for a moment and then started laughing.

"LEAX, you made a joke. You're getting to be more human all the time." LEAX smiled at Hunter and took another drink.

Hunter spoke more seriously. "We were afraid you were dead."

"No, I'm not but, had I moved any more slowly, the B'stri might have changed that outcome."

"The B'stri?" Hunter repeated.

"Yes. He was responsible for the cave-in."

"Was he killed in the cave-in?"

"No."

"Then, how do you know it was him?" LEAX stood up, pulled a small object out of his belt, and handed it to Scott.

"It's our mapRock," Scott told his dad.

"Yes. Apparently, B'stri found it just before we showed up. The cave-in was his way of trying to kill Hunter, protect himself, and keep the mapRock from us."

"How did you manage to get out of the tube alive?" Hunt tried to pose the question subtly.

"When I tripped in the dark, the roof collapse was just beginning to build momentum so not much in the way of heavy rock had fallen yet. The stressors and faults in the lava caused the rock falls to split and go in two different directions. The split left a section of the tube between the two points with marginal rock fall materials. I was in that middle area so only dust and small rock dropped on me. A couple of them really hurt but I figure I got off lucky. After the rock fall stopped, I was able to start looking around. The dust and dirt were very thick in the tube and I had to walk through them to go anywhere. I shined my flashlight around but the air seemed very still and heavy. Then I noticed a slight movement of air back into a side tube. It looked like the dust was being sucked out of the tube. I decided to follow the dust as it flowed back into the darkness."

Hunter and Scott pulled their chairs closer so they could hear LEAX more clearly.

"After walking for several minutes, I heard a sound kind of like the wind blowing through an opening. I felt my way along the wall and managed to find the source of the sound. It was a small opening just about big enough for me to crawl through. I boosted myself up to the opening and started squeezing myself through the hole. I put my hands down on the ground to lever myself through and accidentally touched the mapRock on the ground. I can only guess that B'stri used the tunnel as an exit but dropped the mapRock."

LEAX took another drink of water and settled back in the camp chair.

"We're so happy to see you. Are you hungry?" Hunter asked.

Seeing one of the partially eaten hamburgers, LEAX nodded. "I think I would like one of Scott's hamburgers."

"LEAX, you don't want to do that," Hunter said. "You've been through enough today."

"It's just a good thing I'm cooking tonight," Scott said. "If you were, I'd have to explain the difference between edible food and what you call cooking. If LEAX had to eat your food, he'd want to go back into the tube."

"This is like at the crater?" LEAX asked.

"Yes, LEAX," Scott confirmed. He brought out the hamburger meat and pulled off just enough to make patties for everyone and put them on the fire. When the meat was ready, he opened a hamburger bun, spread mustard and ketchup on it, and put two patties on it.

Scott handed it to his dad who gave it to LEAX.

LEAX ate his burger hungrily.

When LEAX finished, he told Hunt in a voice loud enough for Scott to hear, "We'd better pick up all the scraps. We wouldn't want to make the animals sick." Hunter looked at the two of them and started laughing.

"LEAX, you have no idea what you've started."

Scott looked right at LEAX. "Oh sure, eats one hamburger and now he thinks he's a food critic." Then, Scott put his right hand palm up on top of his left hand. LEAX nodded and returned the sign. Hunter had been listening and watching the scene. He looked at both men and smiled to himself. *It looks like the adventures in the tube had no serious impact on anybody. Everything's almost back to normal.*

"It feels good to just sit down and relax with friends," LEAX said referring for the first time to the growing closeness of their relationship. The smoke from the campfire swirled around providing a wonderful woody aroma that, mixed with the clean pine smell, served to relax everyone. Soon, Scott was dozing.

"Scott, wake up."

He awoke and, for a moment, he was back at a camp out with his dad when all he had to worry about was making sure he doused the fire and made the obligatory remark about his dad's snoring. Then he remembered where he was. He stood, walked to his tent, and climbed into his sleeping bag.

"I think I will call Margie before I go to bed," Hunter remarked. He pushed the familiar numbers on the phone.

"Hunter, is that you?"

"Yeah, it's me, babe." Hunter didn't notice that LEAX was now listening intently to their conversation.

"Hunter, I found it." Margie almost shouted.

"Found what?"

"I found the discrepancy in the time formula that you used in your time travel experiment."

"Really?" Hunt responded, feeling some of Margie's excitement.

"Actually, there were two problems. The empirical formula for the compound was off by a factor of ten and the cocktail was contaminated."

"Wow, you have been busy. I am impressed. If we make those changes, can we make it happen next time?"

"Based on my calculations, we should have the ability to holistically transfer a subject forward or backwards for a controlled amount of time within a year."

"Wow, again," Hunt replied. "I can't wait to try it out."

"So, how are you, Hunt? How is Scotty?"

"We're all well. We spent the night at the zoo in Flagstaff."

"What were you doing there?" Margie inquired.

"We were looking for 'Rocks."

"Haven't you found those things yet?"

"Yes and no," Hunt laughed. "I have so much to tell you when this is all over. We're doing just fine and miss you. Do you want to talk to Scott?"

"Oh, yes."

"Oh, Scotty, your mommy wants to talk to you," Hunter called out in a loud voice. He made sure Scott was awake and then handed him the phone.

"My wife is incredible." Hunt told LEAX as he sat back down.

"Why do you say that?" LEAX leaned forward as if listening intently.

Hunt recapped what had happened when the first transfer occurred.

LEAX stopped him when he talked about the sensory freeze, the headache, and asked, "Did anything like that happen before or since?"

"Nope, just that once for the sensory freeze. However, I have had numerous headaches over the years that seem to be getting worse as I get older."

"Go on with your story."

"We had some problems with the time exchange and could only affect a short term psychological transfer. Margie started analyzing our records and preparations and was able to determine that we had a bad formula and an adulterated solution that may have caused the incomplete transfer." LEAX took a swig of coffee.

There's that strange look again, Hunter told himself.

Hunter continued. "She's amazing with anything to do with DNA. She should be my boss. She's that good." LEAX appeared to be deep in thought.

"That's good to know," he added.

"What do you mean by that?" Hunter wasn't sure what to think of LEAX's comment.

"Oh, just that she's a part of your family that I don't know anything about."

That was a very strange answer.

Hunter suddenly realized how tired he was after just three days on the road.

"Do you recall our last conversation about the Oent'rfazr and the B'stri?" LEAX asked.

"Yes. You said you had something else to tell me."

"What I didn't tell you, Hunter, is that you are also an Oent'rfazr, not a human as you have believed all these years." Hunter snapped upright in his chair as if he'd been shot.

"I'M...WHAT?" His voice trembled as it increased in volume and echoed through the pine trees. He just stared at LEAX. His mouth opened to voice the words but nothing came out. "You get me involved in all this intrigue, require me to deal with strange aliens and Rocks, almost get me killed...several times... and now, you have the effrontery to tell me I'm an alien? That is just not possible." Again, the silence was deafening. As if he were uncertain, Hunter reached slowly for the camp mirror hoping not to see the Creature from the Black Lagoon staring back at him.

Nope, just plain old Hunt, he concluded as he saw his face looking back at him. "Hey, I don't look like LEAX. I look like ... me. I was born in Kecksburg. I have parents. I have friends. I have records of my life." On hearing his own spoken answers, the expression on his face changed to one of great uncertainty. Then, he began again.

"No, I wasn't born in Kecksburg. I don't know where I was born. I have no idea if I even have real parents. There are no records that I existed before 1965." LEAX waited until the import of Hunt's own words sunk in. Then, LEAX and Hunter heard a noise and looked up. Scotty had been standing there listening.

"Since Scott is my son, is he an alien . . . like me?" Hunter asked.

LEAX looked at Scott with uncertainty. "It's hard to tell at this point. Right now, we all need some sleep."

Again, no direct answer. Something just doesn't feel right.

As Hunter reached for the water to drown out the campfire, he felt so many strong emotions— anger, surprise, dread, uncertainty, happiness, and even a sense of peace. Now he understood about his parents, Kecksburg, and his origins. He had a million questions, though. *Were he and Margie still legally married? Was he still a US citizen? What do Oent'rfazr eat . . . people?* But at least he now had an idea about his roots. Hunter thought, *I wonder how Margie will react to being married to an Oent'rfazr? What about Scott?* In the silence of his tent, Hunt thoughts returned to the many things he had wondered about himself for almost all his life. *Admit it. You always felt that this might be a possibility.*

Hunter closed his eyes and fell into a more relaxed sleep than he had since he left Kecksburg.

Dante

The sun was high in the sky. All three men had slept in after the previous day's emotional and physical roller coaster ride. They broke camp quickly, stopped for a fast food breakfast, and got on their way. The discovery last night that Hunter and maybe Scott was Oent'rfazr was still resonating in Hunter's mind. Scott's sighs indicated that he too was still trying to deal with the discovery.

"I'm crossing off the words that we've used and it seems like we're over half way through our adventure."

"I hope that whatever's left goes more smoothly and has fewer surprises than the last three days have had."

"After the tubes, I agree, but we must stay on guard," LEAX agreed.

It was one of those visually spectacular days when they could have been driving in a Monet landscape painting. After the stress at the lava tubes, the pastoral beauty of the drive provided a peaceful reverie.

"This is interesting."

"What did you find, Scott?"

"The next word is *hades*."

"*Hades*? As in hell?"

"I am looking so stay with me."

"What's the next town?" LEAX asked.

"Let's see. It looks like Ashfork."

"What's in Ashfork?"

"It's the Flagstone Capital of the World and . . . wow, they also have a major sinkhole just a bit north of town." LEAX noticed that the Locator was beginning to flash.

"It's reacting and there isn't anything unusual around us."

"Could it be the sinkhole?" Hunt asked.

"I suppose."

"I guess we need to see what is in or around town." Hunt turned the car off the freeway and drove into town. The town was quiet and uncluttered except for the barricades located at the end of Main Street.

"What the heck's going on here?" Scott looked out the car window.

"Let's go find out." They drove down Main until the primary barricade stopped them.

Two burly uniformed men with guns approached the car. "What business do you have here?" one asked.

Hunt thought quickly. "We're tourists and we thought something interesting might be going on."

"This is a secured area. No visitors allowed. You should go back into town to avoid trouble," the other man suggested.

"We'll do that, thanks." Hunter turned the car around and headed back into town. He watched LEAX hold up the Locator, which now was flashing rapidly.

"The mapRock is somewhere in that sealed off area."

"Scott, what did you find on the computer?"

"Hold on, Dad. I am still reading." Hunter found a fast food restaurant and pulled into the parking lot.

"That is something," Scott said.

"What did you find?" LEAX asked.

Noting where they were, Scott asked, "Can I tell you while we eat?"

Scott waited but there was no comment from his dad.

They went inside. Hunt ordered food for everyone and then sat down.

"All right, Scott. What dya find?"

"We just visited Dante's Descent, a natural sink hole that started collapsing over a hundred years ago. It continues to deepen at irregular intervals but the diameter of the hole doesn't seem to change significantly. That would mean…Wait, that's it. That's the connection. We found it. Dante and *hades*. It has to be."

"What do you mean?" LEAX asked.

"In the Middle Ages, a poet named Dante wrote an epic poem called *The Divine Comedy.* It's the story of man's decent through the various levels of hell or hades."

"Looks like you're more than just a pretty face, Scott. Glad we brought you along," Hunter joked. "It makes sense that it contains the next mapRock."

"May contain," LEAX corrected him.

"There's more," Scott added. "This is the first collapse since the fiftieth anniversary of Route 66 in 1976. It's been stable since then. LEAX that should give you your transport point."

"You're learning well, Scott."

"Now, rumors have it that, as they were stabilizing the pit, the crews found something more than they expected and all this effort is to keep people away but not just for their safety."

"Do you think they found the mapRock, LEAX?" Hunter asked.

"Not likely. But, even if they did, it would just seem like a crystalized gemstone to them."

Hunter put his fingertips together in Holmesian fashion. "It looks like we have a problem then. We need to get into the sinkhole to explore for the mapRock but all our accesses are blocked." After a period of silent thought, Hunter asked LEAX, "Can we go back to the time just after the last cave in and look for the mapRock without all the feds?"

"Yes."

"We'll need some very strong flashlights and several long ropes," Hunter noted.

"I'll go see what the town has," Scott offered.

Hunter and LEAX ordered more coffee while they waited for Scott.

"LEAX, how do you deal with the incredible amount of time traveling that you must do? I've only been doing this for three days and I'm feeling the physical and emotional strain big time."

"It's like anything else. You get used to it except for the loneliness that comes from seldom seeing your family." Hunt detected a note of sadness in LEAX's voice.

"When we have some time, I'd like to talk to you about that. Since I, apparently, am an Oent'fazr, I figure it's likely that I'll be time traveling at some point in the future, too."

Just then, Scott came walking back carrying three flashlights and three coils of rope.

"I got all they had."

"Let's get this show on the road," Hunter told Scott and LEAX. They walked back to the car, took out the backpacks, and loaded the gear into them. Then they drove to a more isolated spot nearer the sinkhole and activated the Transporter. They disappeared in the now clichéd swirl of blue color and appeared about a hundred feet from the sinkhole. All the activity and barriers were gone. They had a clear path.

"It looks like we missed the big party," Hunt commented on seeing the clear area. LEAX looked at Hunt, opened his mouth to say something, and stopped. Hunt chuckled.

Atta boy, LEAX, you're getting the hang of it.

The two men reached the edge of the pit and looked down into it. Hunt looked puzzled.

"I thought the article said the pit was three hundred feet deep. That doesn't look like more than thirty feet."

"Do you think it might be the roof of a larger cavern below us since this is a sink hole that we know gets deeper without getting wider?" LEAX asked.

"Anything's possible, I guess."

"If there's a cavern underneath, the mapRock could be in it anywhere." LEAX told Hunter.

"We'd better get down there and see what we can find." They unraveled the ropes, tied them off, and dropped over the side into the hole. When they touched bottom, they started looking around. It was rather non-descript except for a section of the wall that seemed to be a different color than the surrounding wall.

"The only thing I see is that discolored section of wall and the mesh that someone put up to maintain the integrity of the wall. Otherwise, it looks like a typical hole." Hunter started jumping up and down and listening.

LEAX looked at him with a questioning expression.

"No, I haven't lost my mind. I'm checking to see how solid the roof of the cavern is." The lack of an echo indicated the roof was solid.

"I guess we'll have to start with the discolored wall and see where that leads. But, before we do, can you get a quick reading, LEAX?" LEAX checked the Locator and it registered strongly at various locations all around the floor.

"There is no one location where the signal is stronger than in any other place."

"What could be causing that or is the Locator not working?" Hunter asked.

"Could be any number of things especially if there's a cavern below."

"If there is a cavern below and we start digging in the floor, we could cause a cave-in that could injure or kill one or both of us. So, LEAX, maybe we'd better experiment with the wall first so we don't endanger ourselves. Hand me the backpack so I can get the camp shovels out."

Shortly, they were both burrowing into the wall.

"I found something," LEAX called out.

Hunter shined his flashlight beam into the opening.

"It looks like there's a large open area behind the wall."

They enlarged the opening so they could get through and then sat down.

"We have no idea what's ahead of us, how far the opening goes, or how stable it is so here's what I suggest. One of us will stay here; the other will be tethered to the ropes and will follow the opening as far as possible," Hunter suggested.

"I'll try it."

"All right," Hunter told LEAX, "but don't forget to talk to me while you're moving through the openings." They rigged LEAX into a rope harness and he squeezed through the opening. Hunter handed him a flashlight which LEAX promptly turned on and scanned the tunnel.

"Not much in here except it's a part of a larger tunnel that leads away from where you and I are and continues downward."

"Can you follow it without putting yourself in danger?"

"I'll try." Hunter played out the rope as LEAX continued to move down the tunnel.

"Any problems yet?"

"No, the tunnel looks stable. In fact, it almost looks like it was cut into the rock artificially."

"You're at the end of your rope so I'm coming to you now," Hunter told LEAX. He moved cautiously through the hole in the wall and down the tunnel until he saw LEAX's flashlight.

"I see what you mean about the tunnel being cut." He untied the ropes attached to LEAX, and the two of them continued down the tunnel.

"How much further down do you think we have to go, Hunter?"

"I don't know but we must be pretty deep now because I can feel the pressure in my ears." They continued walking until they reached a curve that turned left.

"Dear God," Hunter exclaimed. They found themselves looking at an open cavern so large they couldn't easily see the other side. They played their flashlight beams along all the walls until they both stopped on a small gold-colored, metal structure built into one side of the cavern.

"What's that?" Hunter asked. LEAX pointed the Locator at it and the light got brighter.

"Whatever it is, it looks like it's our destination." They started walking towards the object. When they reached the structure, they noticed it was clean of any markings.

"What is this thing and what's it doing down here?" Hunter passed his hand along the edge as he spoke. They pushed on one of the walls and it opened to reveal a platform with a single slot in one wall and nothing else.

"This gets stranger by the minute," Hunter commented.

"For some reason, this thing seems familiar, like I may've seen it before," LEAX said. "I'm going to leave for a while but I'll be back." He touched the Translator, disappeared, and then, within seconds, materialized beside Hunter.

"What'd you find out?"

"This is a time transport platform that was used by my people for a short time between the end of the flying machine era and the beginning of the Translator era. It had a single purpose– to move Oent'rfazr from one specific point to another specific point and ONLY between those two points. The programmed points could never be changed."

"Great. Do you know where this one goes or even if it still works?"

"No."

"Are we going to try to use it?"

"I think it's the only way to find the mapRock."

"So, we're going somewhere but we don't know where. We don't know how. We don't know if we can get back, and we don't know what it will do to us. Hum, sounds like a typical Hunter Johnson trip." Hunter remembered a similar conversation with Scott.

"If we're going to do this, I better leave Scott a note in case we don't come back." Hunter wrote a short note, put it in his backpack, and left it on the platform. Hunter and LEAX touched the Translator and, after an unusually uncomfortable trip, found themselves in the forested area in the middle of acres of green grass and trees. They obviously were not still in Arizona.

Hunter pointed to the top of a nearby hill. "I don't know why but I think we should go that way." They started walking up the hill looking at the changing colors and smelling the clean air. When they reached the top, they saw a small town. LEAX pointed the Locator at the town and the light increased in intensity.

"Looks like that is where we go." They started walking and within minutes, they were entering the town. Hunter began looking around intently.

"What is it, Hunter?" Hunter continued looking around and then he stopped.

"My God, I know where we are. I…I can't believe it. It just isn't possible."

LEAX listened closely to Hunter.

"This is Kecksburg, my hometown. I grew up here. It looks just like it did then. But how?"

"Perhaps, if we can find 'when', we can answer 'how'," LEAX responded. They went into a nearby convenience store and found a newspaper.

"January 8, 1966." Hunter hesitated. "The crash occurred thirty days ago. That means I…the younger version of me is somewhere around here." He stopped to get control of his emotions. "I need to go to my house."

LEAX stopped him. "There's a chance you might run into yourself while we're here. If you do, you must not be seen by the then-you nor should you attempt any communication with the then-you."

"Why?"

"At the point you make contact with your then-you, you will have changed history for him and consequently for yourself. You'll be creating an event that never happened, which creates a paradox.

In order to reestablish a level time plane and eliminate the paradox, you will cease to exist physically. When that happens, you and any memory of you in the past or future will disappear. Anything you did will be undone, and what you might do in the future will never happen."

Hunter still looked puzzled.

"It means that you and Margie would never have met. Scott would never have been born. Kecksburg would have a significantly different history. This journey would never have happened."

"What would happen to me, physically?"

"You would be injected into a continuous time loop and never be heard from again."

"Wait," Hunter said. "If the person who contacts himself disappears never to be heard from, how do you know what happens in this situation?"

"My people ran different computer simulations at different times with different conditions and information, and in 99.85 percent of the simulations, the effects I described were predicted to happen. Also, several Oent'rfazr were tested and lost. We had a written trail of what each did, and we used time travel to go back and check the events they participated in. Even though we located the time and place, there was no evidence that they had been there. In fact, no one had ever heard of them. We still had the written documentation, but their lives might as well have been a book of fairy tales."

"Did the computers describe what happened to the person?" Hunter asked.

"Yes. At the point in time when the individuals meet, their physical bodies fade out of existence, just as they do now with the Translator. However, the similarity ends there. To understand what happens, it's necessary first to understand how we move through our 'normal' lives. Time is structured somewhat like an infinite 'loaf of sliced bread'. Each slice of bread is an instant of reality. The space in between the bread slices, the cut, is what we call an interstice. The two conditions alternate with one another just like in a loaf of sliced bread. The reality instant is a point in time when we see, hear, feel, touch, taste, and smell the world around us. We're alive or at least we perceive that we exist. At the end of each reality instant, we move into an interstice or gap. This moves us forward an infinitely small amount of time before we 'pop' back into the next adjacent reality instant. While we're in the interstice, we're in sensory limbo. We're not aware of anything about ourselves or our surroundings. In our daily lives, we experience many millions of these movements from reality to interstice and back to reality but we do not remember any of them. However, without them, we would be frozen in time."

"Are the sensory freezes that we experience when we time travel related to moving in the interstices?"

"Yes, Hunter. When we travel using the Translator, we move through the interstices in a kind of wormhole but with an identified end destination where we're 'popped' back out into reality. The individual who experiences seeing himself or herself during time travel is injected into the same wormhole but with no destination. He or she just keeps traveling from interstice to interstice to infinity. If there's an end to infinity and we believe there is, then like a Mobius loop, the individual at the end of infinity will instantly return to the beginning of infinity to complete his journey again. In effect, the person is aware but does not 'exist' long enough for anyone, including himself, to see, hear, feel or be. The individual is truly experiencing a living death."

"Wow. I'm glad you told me. I wouldn't want to lose Margie or Scott because of my curiosity."

"Just remember, our goal is to find the mapRock, get back to Scott, and finish our journey."

"Understood," Hunt responded sounding a bit disappointed. LEAX turned the locator on and it showed a strong reading to the north of town. They started in that direction.

They found themselves in a large wooded area that showed recent activity. A sign that read: UFO crash site ahead. Do not disturb the physical surroundings. US ARMY was the dominant feature in the area.

"The Locator is pointing into that grove of trees," LEAX said. "Let's see what we find." They walked to a large white Oak tree.

"This is where I found the symbol," Hunter remembered. He grabbed a tree limb and started climbing the tree.

"The Locator is on continuously now. The mapRock must be around here somewhere," LEAX told Hunter. He scanned the larger branches as he tried to remember exactly where he found the metal object. He saw a corner of something silver sticking out of a junction of three branches. He reached in and pulled the piece of metal out of the tree. When he did, a small crystalline object dropped out of the tree. Both men's eyes followed it to the ground.

LEAX picked it up. "It's the mapRock." Hunter replaced the piece of metal in the branch and got out of the tree. "I've got to leave myself a note." Hunt found some paper and scribbled a note to himself. When he finished, they walked over to his house and he slipped the note into the mailbox.

"What was that, Hunter?"

"I left a note for myself to look for the metal piece and to hide it. Now we can go. Wait, where are we going? Do you remember where we were?" Hunter asked.

"Not a problem. It was only necessary to know where the booth was programmed to send travelers. We can use the Translator to get back now. I think that somehow the other booth was disabled or destroyed so no one could find it and use it."

They started walking back towards the woods. As they walked down a quiet shaded street, Hunt saw a large black sedan parked on the street. When he passed by, Hunter saw two men sitting there who totally ignored him.

Hunter told LEAX, "There's something about that car."

They continued walking and turned the corner just in time to hear a familiar voice. Hunter and LEAX moved into the bushes to keep anyone from seeing them. They looked across the street as a boy in his late teens stepped up to the door of the house. They heard a male voice say, "Yes, Mrs. Ray, it's me." Then, a female voice said "Are you alone?" The male voice responded, "Yes, Mrs. Ray." Then he went into the house.

"That was me. But if it was, why didn't something happen to both of us, LEAX?"

LEAX replied, "Because the then you didn't see you so nothing has changed in his world." They started moving towards the woods. Just as they got clear of the bushes, the door to the house opened and the then Hunter came out. As he got to the bottom of the steps, he looked over towards the black sedan and saw himself. Hunter tried to keep from looking back at the then Hunter but he couldn't stop the reflex action quickly enough.

"Oh God, no. Not this; not now." His body began to disintegrate immediately. He looked around and saw LEAX reach for his Translator and then fade out. All of a sudden, Hunter was standing in the bushes with LEAX looking at the house.

LEAX told Hunter, "Turn away" when he saw the door to the house open. This time there was no contact and the then Hunter moved quickly out of sight.

"Something feels...different. Did something happen?"

LEAX told Hunter, "I think I accidentally discovered how to save people after they contact themselves."

"What do you mean?"

"When the then you came out the house, you and he saw each other at the same time. You had just begun what I assume was the dissolution process into the other world and your life experiences beginning to disappear. I decided to see what would happen if I went back in time and kept the two of you from looking at each other. I did and it stopped the transition and allowed a re-generation of the primary event before the visual connection."

"Do you mean I was on my way to disappearing permanently?

"Yes. Part of you had already faded. I believe that, if you ask Scott if he felt anything while we were gone, he'll tell you that he had a strange feeling about the same time that you began to disappear."

"Thank you again, my friend."

LEAX nodded. "Let's go somewhere where no one can see us so we can head back to Scott. They found an isolated area near some trees and touched the Translator. Instantly, they were back in the cavern.

"Let's get out of here," Hunter suggested as he grabbed his backpack.

When they entered the tunnel, Hunter told LEAX, "I'm still having issues with why the Kecksburg thing and why now."

"The reason may not be obvious now but maybe by the time the journey is over or maybe it will never be clear," LEAX's voice trailed off. They had begun the ascent to the thirty-foot level but had to stop to catch their breath.

"Just like the explosion crater," LEAX remarked between shallow breaths.

Hunter laughed. "Not quite." Then he got quiet as he remembered the poisoned water and the collapsed mine. They finished the climb and sat down to rest.

Definitely not the crater but tough enough, Hunter thought.

Hunt looked around. "Now, how do we get out of here? I don't think I could hand over hand up a five foot rope let alone a thirty foot one, even on my best day." Then he saw the netting.

"The netting may be our only hope," Hunter told LEAX. They checked out the strength of the netting and determined that it would hold one of them with no problem.

"Let me give this a try." Hunter started climbing erratically. He made it up about ten feet before he stopped, looked back down, and then proclaimed loudly, "I think I can do this." He came back down to talk with LEAX.

"I'll attach the rope to my waist and climb to the top. When I get there, I will tie it off. Then you attach the backpacks to the rope and I will pull them up. Then tie the rope around your waist and I will help pull you up as you climb the netting." Hunter grabbed the netting and began his climb again. Other than a short stop to catch his breath, he made the top quickly. He pulled up the backpacks and then helped LEAX as he climbed up the netting. After LEAX was out, they both looked back down into the hole in silence.

"Hunt and LEAX touched the Transporter and they were back with Scott.

"Are you guys, all right? You weren't gone very long."

Hunter nodded. "You won't believe what we found." While they were walking back to the car, Hunt told Scott the entire story emphasizing Kecksburg and the note.

"What was in the note, Dad?"

"I told my then self to check in the tree for the piece of metal and to keep it in hiding until someone could tell him . . .me what it meant."

"Do you remember getting that note when you were living in Kecksburg?"

Hunter thought for a time. "I'm not sure, LEAX."

I wonder what I would say to myself if I had the same opportunity? Scott asked himself. Shortly, they were at the car. They stored the gear and headed back to the Mother Road.

The Caverns

After recovering from the discoveries at the lava tube and the unexpected side trip to Kecksburg through the sinkhole, they were driving along one of the longest remaining segments of the original Route 66. Scott opened his now tattered list and slid his finger down the page. "Does anyone know what *antre* means?"

Hunter tossed out one of his favorite sayings. "When all else fails..."

"Yeah, I know, I know. Look it up in the dictionary." Scott checked on the Internet. "Ah, it's an old French word meaning cave or cavern."

"Didn't we have the word *cave* before?"

"Remember the gray man?" LEAX reminded Hunter

"Yeah, right," Hunter acknowledged.

"*Caves. Mines. Caverns.*" Scott repeated the words as if hearing them again would help him identify a location. He looked at the list a third time.

Maybe we're going about this all wrong. Scott started thinking about all the caves in the northern part of the state. *There were the ice caves in Flagstaff. The lava caves where they dealt with the cave-in. The cave of time near Sedona. The extraterrestrial cave near Kingman. The Apache Death Cave near Two Guns.* Then he saw a billboard for the Grand Canyon Caverns.

"Listen to this, guys. The Grand Canyon Caverns is a series of very large, connected dry caves that were initially discovered by Jacques Lefrenere, a French immigrant in the late 1880s. The caves are so large that they remain virtually unexplored to this day. One part of the caverns runs northward for nearly fifty miles before opening into the Grand Canyon."

"Sure hope this isn't one of the places where we have to walk a million miles and then find out the mapRock is missing," Hunter told LEAX.

"Because it was a Native American burial ground before it was opened to the public and because twenty-six people have been lost or killed in the cavern, including one woman who hanged herself, the ghost stories about the caverns abound."

"More ghosts? I am beginning to feel like Dr. Vinckman," Hunter joked.

"If you would like to be alone to check out the spirits, there's a unique hotel room located two hundred and twenty feet down where guests can spend the night in the world of the spirits totally cut off from the living."

"Sounds like our kind of place," Hunter noted as he turned off the Mother Road at the sign that read: Grand Canyon Caverns. He pulled around in a half circle and stopped the car next to a large, emaciated, green Tyrannosaurus Rex.

"Okay, what now?" Scott looked at LEAX.

LEAX took out the Locator and began to scan it. It seemed to register strongest when pointed in the general area of a large red sign at the end of a dirt road leading away from the dinosaur. Sloppily painted white letters akimbo on a red background read: Entrance to Grand Canyon Caverns 1/8 of a mile this way.

"I think we can safely say that the Oent'fazr were here and left a mapRock somewhere in the immediate area," LEAX concluded. Hunt drove the car up to an old building that had an obscenely large sign welcoming them to the Caverns and advising them in huge orange fluorescent letters atop an even larger fluorescent pink arrow that the door under the sign was the entrance to the caverns.

"I think we're here but I wonder where we go in?" Hunter asked in his most innocent voice. LEAX started to point at the sign when Scott tapped him on the shoulder and shook his head.

"Let's see if he can find it by himself," Scott told LEAX. *He just never quits.*

The three got out of the car and stretched. LEAX took a quick reading and noted the response was more pronounced than it had been when they entered the property. Opening the door, they walked into a sea of rocks, crystals, maps, old pictures, surveying equipment, and markers located on tables, in display boxes, on the wall, and in cardboard boxes sitting on the floor.

"Look at all this stuff. I used to love coming into these places when I was a little kid," Scott remarked with a broad smile. Clocks, pen holders, picture frames made out of native rocks, not to mention the mandatory tourist staples of rubber snakes, spiders, scorpions in clear plastic, tomahawks, drums and Indian headdresses were interspersed everywhere. He picked up a rubber tomahawk and his eyes twinkled as he relived a childhood memory. They went along a small walkway that led to a large counter with maps on the wall behind it and an old cash register. The sign below the cash register read: Buy admission ticket here.

Scott put his hand on his dad's shoulder. "Don't do it, Dad. Just leave it." Hunter smiled at Scott's remark.

He never changes Scott told himself, shaking his head.

Several tourists milled impatiently around the counter when an elderly woman clad in a khaki shirt and shorts walked up to the counter and began her speech. Her voice was monotone and her eyes darted around focusing on nothing in particular.

Hunter nudged Scott. "How many thousands times do you think she's said those exact words?"

When she finished, the tourists got in line to buy tickets. After purchasing their tickets, LEAX and Hunter sat down.

"Where's Scott?" They looked around and saw him talking to the security guard.

A muffled voice announced, "Group 5A, please report to the elevator." Ten people including the trio formed a queue. LEAX, Hunter, and Scott completed the check in process and rode the elevator to the bottom of the cavern. They found themselves in a large, dimly lit open area where fine dirt, almost the consistency of dust, covered everything. Its muted, almost unearthly appearance produced smothering claustrophobic sensations.

"Not quite what I expected," LEAX said. Visitors looked around the dark recesses that surrounded them creating their own horror story in their minds about what they were going to find or, more likely, what would find them. LEAX and Scott looked for Hunter and saw him in the middle of the people who rode the elevator down with them. Hunter appeared to be listening to the man standing next to him.

"Yeah, boy, you know we have a lot of caves like this back home along the Mississippi. Lots of history in them, too. You know one of those caves is where Mark Twain hung out as a kid and wrote about in his book, *Tom Sawyer*. You know, I bet you don't have anything like that here." Hunt tried to pull away to get to LEAX and Scott but the guy just wouldn't shut up.

"Yup, ol' Mark Twain. You know his real name was Sam Clemens. You know, he was quite a writer. Why I used to work with his grandson and, you know, I got to go to Twain's house and see his room and his writing desk."

"Really?" Hunter commented trying to feign interest.

"Yeah. Ya know, it's really something to see a real famous person like Twain up close, like I did." Hunter chose not bring up the fact that Twain died over a hundred years ago.

When the guy stopped to catch his breath, Hunter started on the offensive. "You know, I had dinner with the President and his wife when I received my Medal of Freedom. I also met George Lucas. He produced Star Wars, you know, and Harrison Ford. Then, I met William Shatner and Leonard Nimoy. They played on Star Trek, you know. Had coffee with Leonard in the cafeteria and he invited me to the set of the new Star Trek movie."

The tourist just looked dumbstruck. "I think I hear my wife calling me.

So long." Hunt exhaled with pronounced finality and began walking toward LEAX.

"If everyone will gather around, we will get started," the guide announced. "There are no living creatures of any kind anywhere in the cave so do not be worried about getting bitten or stepping on an animal."

"What trail will we be going on?" Hunter questioned the guide.

"The extended trail," the guide responded.

Just before they started walking, Scott told Hunter, "I have an idea that I need to talk to the guard about. I am going back up top. I will see you in the lobby." They started walking the trail while everyone else was waiting for the second elevator. LEAX pulled out the Locator and began scanning as they walked. The light got brighter and the frequency of flashing increased as they approached a small natural arch about five hundred feet from the elevator. As they approached the arch, something shadowy moved parallel to Hunter for several seconds and then disappeared.

"Did you see that, LEAX?"

"See what?"

"Naw, I couldn't have seen that. It's impossible."

"Whatever you saw, it must have been your imagination. I didn't see anything. Now we need to get back to the elevator." LEAX started walking very quickly but Hunter seemed to be frozen to his spot.

"Come on, Hunter, hurry."

Hunter looked around and slowly started walking towards LEAX. They pushed as hard they dared in the darkness and just managed to get to the elevator when the door opened and the next group came walking out.

"Are you all right?" the guide stared at Hunter. "You look white as a ghost."

"I...think so."

LEAX was staring at Hunter. "What did you think you saw?"

"I saw what looked like a very large dog but with a body like a —"

"Like a what?" LEAX intoned in an impatient voice.

"A very large . . . scorpion." He pronounced the words slowly and distinctly.

LEAX got that look of concern on his face again. "Did you feel anything?"

"Like what?"

"Like a pin prick or wetness?"

"No, I don't think so." LEAX looked off down the trail and then at Hunt.

"I guess maybe you were imagining it. After all, they said no life of any kind exists in the cavern."

LEAX didn't say that very convincingly, Hunt thought.

The guide was ready to go so they began walking along the path.

LEAX told Hunter, "Let's work our way to the rear of the group so that I can scan for the mapRock. Hunter noticed that this time LEAX spent as much time looking at either side of the trail and peering into crevices as he did looking at the Locator. He got the same reaction at the arch as before but, as they were leaving, the intensity and color began to increase.

LEAX noted, "The mapRock is somewhere beyond the arch." They continued until the tour was completed. They walked back to the boarding area, climbed into the elevator, and rode to the top.

"Do you see Scott anywhere, LEAX?"

"No, where do you think he might be?"

"I don't know, but we better wait here until we find him or he finds us." In a few moments, they spotted Scott walking toward them. The satisfied look on his face told them that he had some good news.

"Okay, guys, I have been talking to one of the security guards while you were goofing off, but, before I enlighten you, did you find the 'Rock?"

Hunter answered, "We know the approximate location in the cavern but we didn't find it. We didn't have enough time because there were people all around us every minute we were there."

"What are you going to do?" Scott inquired.

"We really haven't had time to discuss it."

"Let me tell you how you can make it a clean, smooth operation, if you can run faster than my dad drives," Scott said jokingly.

"At approximately five o'clock, the guard checks with the front desk to see if everyone have come out of the cavern. When he believes that everyone is out, he goes into the caverns and searches along each trail. Then he returns to the surface and completes his daily paperwork."

"What does that have to with us finding the mapRock and getting out?" Hunt questioned.

Scott commented in a slightly peevish tone, "If you wait until he goes down for his final walk through and then go down when he's walking the trails, you should have all the privacy you need. When he gets back into the elevator, you can start actively searching for the mapRock.

"How much time will we have?" LEAX asked.

"Not a problem since for the last few weeks, they have been leaving all the inside entrances and exits open."

"That's good to know."

Scott continued, "When he returns to the top floor from his closing walk through, it takes him about fifteen minutes to finish his paperwork. Then he closes the building and goes home. Once he has gone, you'll have all night to locate the mapRock and then come up to the main floor and you only have to jimmy the outside lock to get out of the building."

"Not bad," Hunter remarked. "It could work."

"Just remember though," Scott warned, "if something happens to you down there, there is no way I can get you help."

"Ok, what do we do until closing?"

"I think I know the answer to that question and you shouldn't have asked it," Hunt cautioned LEAX.

"We need to leave here so we don't arouse any suspicion. There's a small town about five miles from here. Let's go there and kill some time out of everyone's sight," Scott suggested

The three of them went to the car and got in quickly and quietly to avoid being obvious. Hunter drove onto the main road and headed west into the setting sun. They drove until they found themselves in the small, picturesque town of Peach Springs, where they located the only restaurant in town and pulled into the parking lot.

Hunter parked the car and the three of them got out and opened the front door of the restaurant. White peeling paint covered the splintered wooden panels and a chipped, white oval door handle that wobbled from side to side highlighted the door. It looked like the old photos of late 19th century ghost towns they had seen along their journey.

"Looks like this is a good place to sit," Hunter motioned to a nearby table. They sat down at a bare wooden table that was etched with multicolored stains and small holes where knotholes had disintegrated over time. The mismatched wooden chairs seemed to rock unsteadily to an unheard tune.

Hunt looked closely at a clouded, plastic covered menu and told the waitress, "I'm having a double chicken sandwich and an order of fries."

LEAX asked, "Can I have a cheeseburger?"

Scott pondered a second, as if deciding to do what he was thinking about. *Why not,* he thought.

"Do I want three or six double chili cheeseburgers?" he said loudly. He stole a surreptitious glance at his dad to see if his order had the desired effect.

"Good grief," Hunter groaned.

Scott chuckled and confirmed, *Yup, it had the desired effect.* He then asked the waitress, "Is it possible to get three grilled ham and cheese sandwiches?"

The waitress finished writing everything down and walked away indifferent to what had just occurred, as if it happened all the time.

"I don't have a good feeling about this. There are too many unknowns and not enough fall back options, if we get into trouble."

LEAX interjected, "I think Scott gave us a plan that minimizes most, if not all, of those unknowns."

"Yeah," reflected Hunter, "but that great plan didn't tell us what to do if we come face-to-face with the scorpion thing, again."

LEAX's expression didn't match the tone in his voice. "Hunter, you were probably just seeing things after so many potential accidents."

"I would just as soon not see that thing ever again for any reason," Hunter emphasized his words by shaking his head.

Scott looked at his dad, "What scorpion thing?"

LEAX interjected quickly before Hunter could respond. "Your dad just thought he saw an animal that he says looked like a large scorpion."

"What?" Scott exclaimed.

"I just thought I saw something moving in the dark," Hunter added. The waitress bringing the food provided a needed change in the direction the conversation was going.

"I didn't realize how hungry I was," Hunter concluded. They finished their meal quickly and then got up from the table and left payment on the cash register. They walked out of the restaurant and got into the car. Hunter started to put the key in the ignition and stopped.

"Seriously, what're we going to do if we can't get out of the cavern tonight?"

"We'll just have to deal with it if it happens," LEAX responded.

Hunt started the car and pulled out onto the old highway. The sun, focused by the back window, cast a dying spotlight on the back on the three occupants' necks. The green Jurassic sentinel roared at them in practiced silence as they pulled into the caverns parking lot and went inside.

"I guess it's now or never," Hunt said quietly. A few tourists milled around as Scott, Hunter, and LEAX wandered around trying to appear inconspicuous. Hunter was nonchalantly looking at the yellowing newspaper clippings about the caverns on the walls when he stopped abruptly causing the tourist walking behind him to run into him with such force that he shoved him into one of the columns.

"I am terribly sorry," the tourist began. "Are you all right?"

"I think so," Hunter responded. "Sorry, my fault for stopping so quickly. Are you okay?" The tourist nodded yes, gave him one last glance, and walked away. Hunter looked around for LEAX and spotted him near the cash register.

"LEAX." Hunter shouted in that loud whisper voice that you use when you want your voice to carry but don't want anyone but the person you're calling to hear it. "LEAX." he repeated. LEAX hurried over to where Hunter was.

"What?"

"Look." Hunter spun LEAX around so that he could follow his pointing finger. "Right there on the wall."

LEAX followed his finger to a yellowing newspaper article that had a picture that looked like something a Hollywood creature designer would produce in a bad nightmare. It had a translucent shell not unlike that left by a snake after a growth period except this was much larger and more visually descriptive of the shape of the animal it came from. The creature was the size of a large dog but with six jointed legs, three pincher claws, four eyes, and a long jointed tail with two needle-like points arched over its head.

"Is this what you think you saw?"

Hunter swallowed and responded, "Yes, that is exactly what I saw in the cavern when we were there. Is that the product of my imagination, LEAX?"

There was fear evident in Hunter's voice as he began reading the story under the picture. "This exoskeleton was found at the bottom of Grand Canyon Caverns near the old entrance approximately ten years ago. No one has been able to identify what it came from. Several full scale searches have been conducted using the latest technology including infrared, sonar, and motion detectors but nothing has been found living in the cave."

"I wonder how many people think this is a tourist gimmick… not including me?" Hunter pondered.

"It's possible that whatever came out of it died and fell into one of the crevices or that the creature sought refuge in the caverns during its molting and then returned to the outside. Owners have set baited traps throughout the caverns for years but every effort has come up empty."

"That is what I saw. It's still very much alive, regardless of what the article says, isn't it, LEAX?" Hunter's statement was more of a declaration than a question.

LEAX resigned himself to responding. "I recognized the shell as belonging to a highly venomous creature created by the B'stri. Any contact with its venom whether by sting or just contact is lethal within five minutes and there is no known antidote. More proof that the B'stri is continuing to try to bring about your death."

Hunt thought about the creature and exclaimed, "We have to be much more careful from now on then."

"Look, there goes the guard down the elevator. We need to get ready to go, Hunter." They watched the guard disappear as they checked their watches.

The minutes passed slowly until Hunt finally whispered, "Let's go." They walked to the elevator, checked to see if anyone was watching them, and then got in. Hunt pushed the button marked 'cavern' and the elevator began its slow descent.

"If the guard is still there when we get to the bottom, let me do the talking," Hunt admonished LEAX. "Also, move to the side of the door when it opens so that if the guard just takes a quick look, he may not see us." They looked at each other apprehensively as the elevator came to a stop. In the few moments between the time the elevator stopped and the door opened, both men tensed visibly. Then the door opened.

Hunt looked out the elevator door. "He's gone. Let's go." They moved quickly to the first trail marker and started down the trail.

"Listen," Hunter told LEAX. They heard a noise coming from the darkness and then saw more shadowy movements against the low lighting. It was the sound of modern music and the guard's voice trying to sing along. It grew fainter indicating he was moving away from them.

"At least we'll know if he's getting close to us." The two started walking again until they found the arch, where they had gotten the reading earlier in the day. LEAX pulled out the Locator and started scanning the area. Within seconds, it locked on.

"Look around for any unusual sign or marking," LEAX suggested. They started shining their flashlights on the arch. There was a piece of rock that looked like a large triangle near the left side of the arch.

"This will be our reference point," LEAX indicated, as he estimated the distance to the triangle. Because we're inside in the dark, we need to make sure we have an accurate way to measure what references we do have." Hunter and LEAX both touched the Translator at the same time and in moments, they reappeared in the darkened cavern.

Hunt shined his flashlight beam on the arch. "There it is." LEAX took out the Locator and found the mapRock buried just under the arch. They dug through the hardened soil and located the box with the mapRock in it. They picked up the box, buried it under the triangle-shaped rock so they would know exactly where it was in the present, and then they touched the Translator. The transition was instantaneous.

"I am finally getting used to all the time travel. I don't feel any of the effects anymore."

They started looking and listening for the guard.

"Do you hear any music?" Hunter asked LEAX.

"None," LEAX shot back as he began moving toward the elevator. Hunter was not far behind. When they reached the landing platform, Hunter pushed the up button and stepped back. The lights didn't come on nor was there any mechanical noise. He pushed the button repeatedly and still nothing happened. Then, he announced with great finality, "Great. We're locked in."

"So much for unlocked doors." LEAX then posed the question that no one expected to hear. "What do we do now?"

"We have to get out of here without being seen," Hunt stated as he turned on his flashlight and started playing it all around the floor. He stopped at a sign that read: Cavern Bedroom this way.

"What is that, Hunter?" They started walking in that direction. After going about two hundred feet, they saw multicolored lights that illuminated a small area named the Crystal Room.

"Can you believe this?" Hunter asked. In the cavern on a large wooden platform was a full size bed, a couch, a table with chairs, a table, an entertainment center, a large rug, a kitchenette with electrical appliances, a refrigerator, and a bathroom. Hunter looked around for several minutes.

"I don't know about you, LEAX, but I am hungry and thirsty." He opened the refrigerator and found two bottles of water. He brought the water to the table where LEAX was. "We have two serious problems that need solutions or at a least a plan. We need to find the mapRock and we need to get out of here as soon as possible. The map in the lobby showed that there was an alternate way in and out when the caverns were first opened but that entry was now sealed. We can walk the different paths until we find something that looks like it could have been an opening or until we're convinced there's no other way out and we have to wait until morning."

LEAX nodded. "I suggest that we start with the pathway that leads to the arch so we can grab the mapRock on our way to find the opening." The two started walking back into the darkness. As they walked further, Hunt was looking all around watching for whatever it was that he had seen before. It had scared the living daylight out of him and it wasn't anything he wanted to sneak up on him.

"Shouldn't we be getting close?" Hunt asked. They walked along the path until they came to the arch where they reburied the box. LEAX looked up, scanned his light across the rock, and stopped at the rock triangle on the wall.

"Let's see if we can find the 'Rock so we can get out of here," LEAX told Hunter.

This time the Locator didn't register above a very slow, barely visible light emission. While LEAX was checking the Locator, Hunter yelled, "What was that?"

Hunter, trying to get control of his jitters, told LEAX, "I heard some rocks falling that started on the other side of the path and then got louder." They both stopped talking and started looking and listening as they scanned the area with the flashlights.

"I don't see anything," Hunter responded quietly. "Do you?" Just as LEAX started to respond, he stopped suddenly.

Hunter started to ask but LEAX held up his hand. "Be quiet."

Both men waited for several seconds and then they heard raspy, guttural breathing and then a low scream that reminded Hunter of the videos he had seen when a predator in the wild was closing in for a blood kill. He felt his body begin to shiver uncontrollably. Hunter watched LEAX, who was slowly reaching into his belt.

"What're you doing?" Hunt asked.

Again, LEAX signaled Hunter, "Be Quiet. Our lives depend on it." The darkness of the cavern kept them from seeing anything clearly but they could tell from the sounds that something was circling them like an animal closing for the kill. Suddenly, a stench like nothing Hunt had ever smelled before blasted his nostrils.

What is that godawful smell? he thought. With instincts remnant of a past where fighting for survival was a daily necessity, both men pivoted around in small circles trying to keep whatever it was directly in front of them. Suddenly, all sound stopped. They looked around but couldn't see or hear anything.

"Where is it?" Hunt asked. In the dark, feeling the total helplessness that comes with no control, no awareness, and not knowing one's fate, Hunter began to believe that he was going to die. The growling began again only this time it was much closer and behind them.

Hunter yelled out without thinking, "Behind you, LEAX." Then, he realized that he had just given his location away to the animal. Hunter could feel his heart thumping in his throat. The thing began circling again and this time they could hear movement and falling rock. Hunter could see that LEAX was dropping into a squatting position.

He signaled Hunter from about five feet away just above a whisper, "When I yell, you run towards me as fast as you can and run by me on my left side. On my left side as fast as you can," he repeated, lifting his left arm to emphasize his instructions

Hunter mouthed the word 'yes' as if he understood why he was saying that. The sound began getting closer and, at one point, Hunter shined his flashlight in the direction of the noise just in time to see six jointed, translucent legs attached to an elongated blood red translucent body that looked like decaying meat. Three large pinchers and a segmented tail displaying stingers that looked like two long hypodermic needles extended from the body. Then, it blended back into the darkness.

Hunter commented in a disconnected voice, "That picture in the lobby didn't do this thing justice." They heard something on the top of a small ledge just in front of Hunter. He flashed his light and looked up to see four evil looking, dead black bulging eyes above a number of long white fangs jutting out of a drooling mouth. Hunter instinctively backed up and, when he did, he noticed that LEAX had repositioned himself in a direct line with the creature and him.

I wonder why LEAX did that? Hunter thought.

The grotesque legs moved in articulated rhythm as the tail twitched back and forth as if practicing for the death stroke. The mouth opened and closed in a scissor-like motion dripping blood saliva on the ground. It was then Hunter realized that the animal was stalking him.

I am trapped. When he stepped to the left, the animal moved to his left with him. The dead black eyes seemed to follow even Hunter's smallest movement. *Well, I don't see many ways out of this. I only hope it will be quick and painless.* He had already accepted that his life was forfeit. The animal was slowly crouching into a primal springing position.

Just at that moment, LEAX shouted, "RUN", at the top of his lungs, to Hunter, who turned and ran to LEAX's left. At the same time, the animal sprang forward with such ferocity and speed that it nearly landed on Hunter's back where it would have been only seconds to the kill. It would reach Hunter in seconds.

In a final instinctive reaction, Hunter yelled, "LEAX".

In the split second after Hunter yelled, LEAX raised the Translator, braced himself, and buried it with all his strength against the body of the incoming animal. The impact was so strong that, even though LEAX had prepared himself for it, it jarred him and shoved him backwards with such force that he broke a section of the stone arch when he fell.

LEAX cried out, "Aaaaaaarggghh". He felt the pain of the impact and then everything went dark. He didn't see the animal become encased in the swirling blue light and disappear somewhere into the past. As he ran past LEAX, Hunter collapsed face down on the cavern floor. He saw the glow of the blue light illuminate the area and then fade into the darkness. He looked around for LEAX and saw him on the ground.

Hunter asked, "Are you hurt?" When he didn't answer, Hunter slowly got up, limped over to him, and extended a hand. LEAX's eyes fluttered momentarily and then he looked up at Hunter, grabbed his extended hand, and pulled himself up. They stood there motionless still grasping hands as they fought to regain their mental and physical control. Without thinking, Hunter grabbed LEAX. "Thank you, my friend."

Hunter stared at the spot where the animal vanished. "Was that what you thought it was?"

LEAX picked up his Translator. "Yes. That was a B'stri hunting animal. Among other things, the B'stri like to kill animals in the cruelest way possible. They created these animals to help them in that task. Their poison paralyzes on contact and within a short time, it begins to decompose the victim's body into a gelatin. They're alive during that change so the B'stri, in a final act of cruelty, set fire to the still living remains. The process is painful and is purely for the animal pleasure of the B'stri. It didn't take them long to find out that it worked equally well on their enemies."

"Would that have happened to me if he had gotten the poison on or in me?" LEAX nodded his head slowly up and down.

"I owe you my life. Thank you." After a moment of silence, he asked, "Would that could have happened to you if the thing had accidentally splashed any venom on you while you were helping me?"

LEAX nodded again. The two men stood where they were for a few minutes just looking around without saying anything.

A Way Out

"We probably should get started," LEAX told Hunter. They picked up the flashlights and started toward the arch.

"You know, LEAX, we know about where the mapRock is but we have no idea about the exit out of here. Maybe we should start looking for the exit first and then come back and get the mapRock later."

"Worth a try."

"This seems like a good place to start looking. We can follow the path to its end and then come back. Let's see, it's almost eight o'clock so that means we have been down here for over three hours. We should try to call Scott." The phone buzzed several times and then it stopped. Hunter looked and his battery was almost dead.

"I guess we won't be talking to anyone tonight. I wonder if the texting still works?" Hunter began the text: "Locked in cavern. Looking for original entrance. See if you can find the original entrance out there." He pressed send and told LEAX, "Now, we wait."

"Let's hope he gets it."

"Here it comes now." Hunter read: "Looking."

"Let us know."

"Another message coming."

Hunter read: "You and LEAX, okay?"

"For now."

"Let's go," LEAX responded. The two of them began walking down the path. In the darkened area, they moved more slowly, this time to keep from tripping.

After several minutes of silence, Hunter asked, "You started to describe your family earlier. What are your lives like? Are they like ours?"

"Yes and no."

"That sounds like a good place to start the conversation."

"Our main difference is that you humans are three dimensional beings, who exist in a three dimensional world, mostly under your control. You can choose to move left and right, forward and backwards, and up and down but you're locked into a common time slice." Hunt strained to understand what LEAX was saying.

"When time moves, you have no choice. You must move with it. You remain in the same three dimensional space as those who are with you, even as time passes."

"Yeah, that's true…for now," Hunt concurred. "How are we different there?"

"We Oent'rfazr are four dimensional hyperbeing beings, who can exist in the three dimensions just as you do but, by choice, we can also exist and move through the fourth dimension. We can move independently in all four dimensions. Just the opposite of you."

"I am not sure I follow you, LEAX."

"What that means is that we can all be sitting in one room and then one of us decides that we need to go forward or backward and we just do it. When we do move in that fourth dimension, we become invisible to those remaining behind because we no longer exist in that specific time frame. So much of our lives are spent outside each other's presence even though we may still be in the same room or different rooms."

"Wow, even after that good explanation, I'm not sure I fully understand what all that meant."

They continued walking in silence for several minutes. Then Hunter called out another topic. "Let's try something a little easier for me. What kind of books do you have? Are they mostly about time travel?"

"We have been building a virtual library to improve our knowledge access and also to help our young ones become more familiar with time travel, sort of passing the torch, as you might say. Our goal is to make books unnecessary for the next generation."

"Unnecessary? How will you teach your children? How will you pass on history?"

"With the new educational infrastructure being built, teachers with their classes or kids by themselves beyond a certain age will be able to travel to an event they are studying and watch it actually happen where it happened. Much as we have done on this journey."

"But what about the other things that books provide? They aren't just about events. They offer a look at the conditions leading up to the event and the effects of the event on the present and the future."

"In our world, facts are most important. The learner will build his or her own understanding of history based on the scope of travel and what the teacher tells him or her. Also, we're working on a method for the traveler to be able to ask questions of the participants in the events before they happen, after they happen, or, in some cases, while the events are occurring."

"I could see how that would make learning more interesting and more complete. What about pets? Do you have any pets?"

"Yes, we're permitted one pet."

"What do you have?"

"The closest thing I can see in your world is a dog."

"What kind?" Hunter asked, thinking about Bill the Bassett.

"There are no kinds. They're all the same. They eat and protect the house."

"Don't you play with them or take them for a walk?"

"No, its job is to guard the house; nothing more."

Just at that moment, the far off sounds of drumming broke the silence in the caverns. Not the type you hear from musical groups but a steady staccato of one note in slow measured rhythm.

LEAX turned. But before he could ask, Hunter said, "I don't know. Let's just keep going." They started walking again listening for any changes to the drumming. After about ten minutes, Hunter said, "I think it's getting louder, LEAX. Does it sound like that to you?"

"Yes," LEAX spoke the word quietly. They continued walking and turned a long sweeping corner that opened into a large open area. The beams from their flashlights shot out but the darkness on the right absorbed them.

Hunter commented, "This must be a very large cavern." They splayed their flashlight beams all around the nearby walls on the left side. Suddenly, the Locator went wild. The flashing was so fast that it seemed like it was one continuous light. They stood there trying to figure out what was happening.

"Listen, it sounds like the drumming is getting louder and faster," Hunter said. "This is getting stranger by the minute." LEAX scanned the wall to their left.

LEAX told Hunter, "Shine your light up there." He pointed his light where LEAX's light ended.

At the end of the beams was a long rope that had one end tied around a large rock. The interwoven strands of the rope were red and yellow. They followed the rope with the light beams from the rock as it curled around to the other side.

"What is a rope that color doing in this part of the cavern?' LEAX asked. They walked along the path and turned a corner keeping their beams on the rope. When they turned the corner, both men dropped their flashlights.

"Please tell me I'm not seeing this," Hunter told LEAX. A human skull with part of the spinal vertebra still attached hung at the end of the rope. The two slowly regained their composure and picked up the flashlights. The drums, which had stopped briefly, began again, more loudly this time.

"I wonder if that is the remains of the lady who hanged herself down here?"

He looked up at the skeleton again. "A couple more jolts like the ones in the past few hours and I'll be joining that skeleton."

LEAX was pointing the wildly flashing Locator at the ground directly under the skeleton.

"I think we're going to find the mapRock somewhere around here," LEAX commented with some confidence. Hunter picked his courage up off the ground, pulled the small camp shovel out of his belt, and began digging in the sand-like material. The drumming continued and it seemed to be increasing in volume again. Within a few moments, the shovel hit a hard surface and simultaneously the drumming stopped, leaving the two in unexpected silence. Hunt stopped digging and LEAX cleared the sand from around the container. It was one of the boxes that they had found some of the other mapRocks in. LEAX lifted the box out, set it down, and cleaned off the dirt. He opened the box and found the mapRock between a fold of material that LEAX didn't recognize. Hunter held it up and saw that it was a piece of Native American weaving. They both stopped and looked at the mapRock and the weaving.

"I wonder?" Just then, Hunter heard the signal indicating there was a text from Scott.

Hunter read: "Long time since text."

"We're fine, need out of here."

Hunter read: "What do you want me to do?"

"Where are you?"

Hunter read: "Think I found the entrance."

"How do you know?"

Hunter read: "Big sign says Site of the original entrance to the caverns." Hunter just shook his head.

"We will try shining our flashlights around any crevices or openings down here. See if you see any flashes of light."

Hunter read: "All right."

Hunter told LEAX, "Let's just play our flashlight beams all around the cavern."

"Anything?"

Hunter read: "Nothing."

After five minutes, Hunter texted again. "Anything?"

Hunter read: "Nothing"

"It's getting close to eleven, so we better try the other paths, LEAX. Let's head back to the elevator for now."

"Moving to other trail. Talk later."

As they were walking back towards the elevator, Hunter continued the conversation from earlier. "Given how fourth dimensional travel works, how is it affecting your family?"

"What do you mean affecting them?"

"Don't you wish you could spend more time doing things together?'

"My son and I have been finding ways that we can stay together but the B'stri see this as a change to what they want so it's a threat to their future and they want to stop it."

"Their future? Isn't this about the culture and development of the future of YOUR people?"

"Although it sounds restrictive and domineering, they do have rights to protect their culture and their future."

Hunter looked at LEAX. "Wait, aren't these the guys who have been doing everything in their power to kill us? How does that give them rights over you or me?"

LEAX gave Hunter a 'you just don't understand look' and continued. "I attended some meetings of the B'stri to try to understand what their philosophy was about and I understand more than most Oent'rfazr what the B'stri are trying to accomplish and why. As I said, I don't agree with their approaches but their reasoning for their survival is valid and should be considered."

"Yes," Hunter replied, "but having an idealistic goal does not justify using illegal or unethical tactics that do to the other people what you're complaining about. We have a saying, 'Your rights end where my nose begins.'

"As I said, I don't agree with the methods of the B'stri, but I understand why they're the way they are."

Hunter replied, "What do you mean?"

"People have the right not to be intimidated either by threat or by action. They have a right to be who they are."

"Yes, but how does that fit here? They want their freedom to do whatever they want to do and they will do anything to get it including killing others whom they perceive as a threat. That doesn't seem right."

"In the meetings, they told us about many abuses that the Oent'rfazr has heaped on them to keep them 'under control'. That doesn't seem right either."

"Why does that give them the right to try to kill us…me?"

LEAX looked at Hunter. "Your ancestors believed in what the B'stri are trying to do and how they're trying to do it." Shouldn't they have the same rights as your ancestors?"

Hunter's mouth dropped. "What are you talking about? How can you compare a race of blood thirsty killers to a group of people looking for their freedom?"

LEAX began, "Whenever any form of government becomes destructive of these ends, it is the right of the people to alter or abolish it and to institute a new government. But when a long train of abuses and usurpations, pursuing invariably the same object evinces a design to reduce them under absolute despotism, it is their right, it is their duty to throw off such government and to provide new guards for their future security."

Hunter just stood there in abject amazement.

LEAX continued, "Your people had no problem killing other people so that they could have their desired form of government because the existing one was unacceptable."

Hunter listened to LEAX repeat the words from America's birth documents and apply them in a way that contradicted everything they stood for. "How can the B'stri think that these idealistic words give them the right to kill people and destroy other cultures and ways of life to get what they want?"

Hunter looked at LEAX and started to ask if he really believed what he had just said but then thought better of it. Shortly after that, they arrived at the elevator.

"While we were walking, I had a thought. Could you travel back in time to when the cavern was first opened, locate the opening, and then come back here?"

"It can be done but it's very dangerous and unwieldy when the time tie between landings is very short," LEAX responded.

"What do you mean?"

"If you think about it, when we return, we have very specific time references that must be met for us to meet up. If we come back thirty seconds before or after we leave, then we will not link up. We will be out of time synchronization and we will be lost to each other in time."

"We have two choices then," Hunter began. "One is dangerous now and one is dangerous later. If we just wait until the caverns open in the morning, we will be sure to be in synchronization but the B'stri might beat us to the technology. If we travel back to locate the opening, we might lose synchronization and we will have a four dimensional problem that might result in our never finding the technology and maybe each other and the B'stri still achieves their objective."

"Perhaps it's time we influence our future," LEAX stated.

"I'm not willing to risk not seeing my family and friends ever again and that includes you. This is my life and the life of our worlds. I say we stay here, wait it out, and then sneak out tomorrow morning."

"We may be signing the death warrants for ourselves and our worlds," LEAX reminded Hunter.

Hunt shook his head slowly, breathed a deep sigh, and, then with pronounced resignation, said, "The choices we make dictate the life we lead; to thine own self be true."

"What was that?"

"Something a brilliant man wrote many years ago and something Scott and I share." Hunter pulled out his phone and started the text, reading aloud to LEAX as he went.

"Planning to stay the night here and sneak out in the morning. Go back to the car and sleep. When people come in the morning, send us a text, and get everything ready to go." He hesitated thinking about the effect of the text and what they would have to do. Then he continued, "We'll do Butch and Sundance and we'll need you to be outside with the motor running."

LEAX looked perplexed. "Butch and Sundance?"

Hunter smiled. "Do you know what I mean when I say 'haul ass'? You run as fast as you can and meet me outside at the car. Don't stop for anything."

"Yes, I think I understand." From the look on his face, Hunter wasn't sure that he did. He looked at his watch; it was almost midnight. As the excitement and apprehension of the day began to wear off, Hunt realized he was hungry.

"LEAX, are you hungry?"

"Yes, but where's there something to eat down here?"

Hunter stood up. "Follow me."

The two of them walked down the trail. Several minutes later, they came to a very large platform that contained many small, white boxes stacked one on top of the other.

"What's this?" LEAX looked confused.

"This is what reading books will get you. These are the rations that were stored here during the Cuban Missile crisis in 1962 in case there was a nuclear war. There's enough food here to feed two thousand people for over four months." Hunt picked up one of the boxes, pulled out a small pocketknife, and cut open the top of the box. Inside were individual, self-contained meals. He handed one to LEAX, who just looked at it and then at Hunter.

"This is something to eat?" LEAX asked.

Hunt opened the package, took out the small container of water, poured it into the package, and then shook it to reconstitute the food.

"Here we go." He scooped out what looked like a piece of meat and bit off a small piece for taste.

"Boy, I appreciate Margie's peanut butter casserole now more than ever." He put the rest of the meat in his mouth and chewed it. "Umm, it isn't too bad if you can find a way to deaden your taste buds. Try it, LEAX."

LEAX opened the package, poured water into it as he had seen Hunt do, and then rolled it around. He reached in, picked the substance out, carefully put it in his mouth, and bit down.

Hunter watched LEAX chew his food. "What dya think?" While LEAX was trying to figure out if he liked it or if he could possibly eat more, Hunter had opened another container and started eating it.

LEAX opened a second packet.

After his third packet, Hunter was ready to move on. "Now, we can go get some rest." They walked back toward the elevator and then toward the dimly lit area they had seen earlier.

Hunter pointed at it. "All the comforts of home." LEAX collapsed in the stuffed chair and Hunt fell into the recliner.

"I didn't realize how tired I was. We should try to get up about five o'clock and figure out our plan."

LEAX replied, "The Butch and Sundance haul ass?"

Hunter smiled, got up, went to the refrigerator, opened the door, and focused on several silver cans.

"Aha," Hunter exclaimed. "Adult beverages. LEAX, would you like one?" LEAX looked as if he wasn't sure so Hunter popped a top and handed LEAX a beer. Both men took huge first swallows.

Hunter smacked his lips followed by a big "Ahhhhh." LEAX was smacking his lips too but it looked more like he was trying to get the bad taste out of his mouth. The cavern got quiet as the overhead light painted them a silent sterile yellow. Within minutes, Hunter began to doze off but he did notice that LEAX was looking at a device that he had not seen before.

I wonder what that is? I'll have to ask him in the morning.

It looked as if he was reading something. The expression on his face told a story that what he was reading was not pleasant. LEAX put the device down and folded his hands as if were thinking.

Hunter asked, "Is something wrong?" LEAX looked up in surprise.

He didn't say anything for a moment but then commented, "Things are changing and I have to show that I am changing with them or…." He paused.

"Or what?" Hunter prodded for an answer.

"My family" is all LEAX would say. Hunter started to ask and then stopped. *He looks like he needs some space.* In a few moments, Hunter was asleep and LEAX continued just staring at the floor.

At five o'clock, Hunter awoke. He looked around and saw that LEAX was still just staring at the floor.

"Did you get any sleep?"

LEAX jumped with sudden surprise and momentarily revealed a face twisted into a mask of evil proportions. Then the mask was gone. LEAX shook his head as if he suddenly became aware of where he was.

"I'm fine."

Hunter got up and told LEAX, "I am going to wash up while we still have time." When he came out, LEAX was still looking at the floor.

"Are you hungry, my friend?" LEAX nodded and joined Hunter at the table. They shared a breakfast of coffee, fresh fruit, and cream right out of the refrigerator.

At 5:30, he texted Scott. "Any activity up there yet?"

Hunter read: "I just saw a couple of cars drive up and park. Two people got out and went in."

Hunter was getting ready to respond when he received another text.

Hunter read: "Elevator door open. Should be easy to use. Get ready."

"Make sure you're ready," Hunter told LEAX. He checked for the mapRock and the device he was reading last night as well as the flashlights and the Locator.

"I'm ready," he told Hunter. Hunter moved over to the elevator and punched the button. It stayed lit and the sound of the car descending filled the cavern.

"Almost time," Hunt primed LEAX.

"Clear, Scott?"

Scott watched as the two people sat down in the lunchroom with coffee and the paper.

Hunter read: "Go." LEAX and Hunter jumped into the elevator and punched the ground floor button.

At that moment, Scott saw the guard get up and walk towards the end of the building where the elevator was located.

"Damn," Scott murmured. "Not now." He got ready to text his dad to stop the elevator but the guard apparently found what he wanted and started back to the lunchroom. Scott started the car and parked it in front of the building.

"Come on, guys," Scott whispered. "It's time." The elevator stopped and the door opened. Hunt took a quick look and turned to LEAX.

Just as Hunt was ready to say something, LEAX ran past Hunter and, in a quiet but emphatic voice, called out, "Haul ass now." Hunter managed to get up to speed while chuckling and caught up with LEAX. They arched around the corner and it was a straight shot to the door.

They had just about reached the doorway when a voice from the cafeteria shouted, "Hey, who are you?" and then the guard tripped over a chair. It was all the cushion Hunter and LEAX needed. They bolted through the door and outside the building to where Scott had the car running.

"Haul ass," Hunter yelled at Scott. They jumped in and Scott sped off.

Hunter watched behind them but didn't see any pursuers. Within a short time, they were westbound outside of Peach Springs.

"Still no activity," Hunter observed. Scott stopped the car so that he and his dad could trade places.

After they got the car up to speed, Hunter commented, "That was one of the strangest… and spookiest… experiences I have had in a long time and, for this trip, that is saying a lot."

"What do you mean?" Scott asked.

"We heard what sounded like Native American drums echoing throughout the caverns as we got closer to the mapRock and then we saw the lady who hanged herself by the neck with a multicolored rope."

"Wait, you saw the lady who hanged herself?"

"Well, her skeleton anyway."

"That is absolutely impossible."

"Why?" asked Hunter.

"The history of the caverns described the event at some length including who the lady was, what she was wearing, where they found her, and even listed a number of reasons for her taking her own life."

"How does that make our seeing her impossible?"

"They took her body down and buried her in a local Indian cemetery shortly after they found her. They even buried the rope with her."

"A long rope with red and yellow woven strands?" Hunter asked.

"Yeah," Scott replied looking at his dad in a disbelieving manner.

"I am just glad we're out of there, but you know I am still hungry even after the C-rations and fresh fruit," Hunter reflected.

"What?" Scott reacted again. "You ate C-rations and fresh fruit…while you were down there?"

LEAX saw his chance, "And we slept on big comfortable oversized stuffed chairs and a bed, had hot water, and, what did you call it, Hunt? A cold adult beverage?" Scott just looked back and forth between the two of them.

"Gimme a break. You guys think I just fell off the Oent'rfazr truck?"

Mercury

They barely had time to recover from the wild trip out of the caverns when they were preparing for their next destination.

"I sure hope we find the last mapRock soon. I'm not sure I can keep this pace. I feel like I am in my own version of Indiana Jones," Hunter joked.

"What's the next word, Scott?" LEAX asked.

Scott pulled out his list. *Gunfight.* He reached for the 66 roadmap to see what was ahead. They were just west of Peach Springs so the next three sites before Kingman were Truxton, Valentine, and Hackberry. Scott read a quick synopsis of the three towns and found nothing about gunfights.

"It doesn't sound like much of anything happened in these areas," Hunt noted. Scott brought up Doc's book and began reading.

"Wait, here's something else," Scott added. "The next site after Hackberry was a small, now completely leveled site named Mercury. It got its name from a small mercury mine that produced for several years but could never be made commercially successful."

"I didn't know Arizona even had any mercury mines," Hunter interjected.

"Several members of the Clanton gang, who fought it out with the Earps at the OK Corral in Tombstone, had stopped in Mercury earlier on their way to Utah."

"This trip is beginning to feel like a giant, real life history book," Hunter commented.

Scott continued, "Most of the town's cowboys were gone leaving only a few men to protect the town—really only a saloon, the cattle company office, which doubled as a small bank, and several bunk houses. On the way north, the gang heard that there was a lot of money in the town from the last large shipment of cattle."

"Let me guess. They robbed the bank?" Hunter asked.

"Yeah, that is exactly what they did but they failed to get away quickly enough and wound up being pinned in a shed at the corral by a number of the townspeople. It turned out to be a wait out rather than a shootout but after about five hours, the gang decided to make a run for it. The citizens waiting outside cut most of them down.

"What happened?" LEAX asked.

The Clantons escaped but all the rest were killed and several even managed to fall into the old mine, as they were staggering around after being hit by a hail of bullets. All that remains at the site now is a small portion of the corral fence that, unlike most other corrals, was made of adobe rather than barbed wire or wood. And somewhere in the area is the sealed opening to the old mercury mine."

"Now, if we could just figure out where the town was," Hunt said, "we'd be all set."

Scott had developed a process along the way that allowed him to isolate possible locations more quickly.

"Let's see, the last confirmed dream list item was *cave*, which was the cavern. The next word is *gunfight* and then *abomb*. There are no additional sites between here and Kingman so let's assume that Mercury is our choice." After several minutes more of looking, Scott announced, "Guys, I don't know about Mercury. Even ole doc doesn't have any site location information in his book."

Hunt glanced to his right. "LEAX, I will say that if your people were trying to make it difficult to find what they hid, they should be getting a gold medal for this little dandy."

Scott was flipping through the pages of Doc's book when he came up with an idea. "I think I might have a solution but it's a long shot."

"When you have nothing else, a long shot is definitely the best choice," Hunter told him. Scott punched in a number.

"Who're you calling?" LEAX asked.

Scott looked down at the computer for a moment and then said, "Hello?"

LEAX looked at Hunter in a quizzical manner and Hunt just shrugged his shoulders.

"Hello," Scott repeated in a more positive voice. "My name is Scott Johnson and I'm reading, well, actually using your book on a journey I am on along Route 66. It has been an incredible resource and a lifesaver in several situations."

The voice on the other end responded, "Thank you."

"In fact, we're on that journey right now and are at an impasse that even your book doesn't seem to have any information about."

"Where are you and what is the impasse?" Scott looked up and gave the thumbs up sign.

"We're east of Kingman and looking for Mercury."

There was a deep sigh on the other end of the phone and an extended silence. "Hello?" Scott said again.

"That was probably the hardest place along Route 66 to find any information about, let alone the actual location."

"Did you ever find the actual location?"

"I was not able to find information that pinpointed where it was so I went out looking myself when I was writing 'Ghosts'. You would think it would be easy to find. However, I did locate a very small section of adobe wall south of 66 that I think might have been Mercury but I couldn't find anything to corroborate it so I chose not to identify it as Mercury."

Scott's voice reflected his growing excitement. "Do you think you could give me directions to where you found the wall?"

"Let me look through my notes and see what I can find. Can I call you back at this number?" the voice asked.

"You bet," Scott replied, barely able to contain his enthusiasm.

"Who was that?" his dad asked.

Scott smiled. "Doc Lee."

"Where'd you get his number?"

"It was on the back page of his book."

"What did you find out?" Hunter asked.

"He thinks he may have located a segment of the corral where the gunfight might have taken place but he isn't sure. He couldn't validate it so he didn't put it in his book. He's checking his records of that day."

"Wow," LEAX reacted emphatically and both Scott and Hunter stared at him.

"Did I do that right?" Scott put his right hand palm up on top of his left hand.

"What do we do now?" Hunt posed the question to Scott.

"Doc is going to call me back later so it looks like we have some time to be tourists. There's a small store at Hackberry. Let's go get something to wet our whistle … to drink, that is…while we're waiting for Doc's call," Scott suggested.

Hunt started the car, turned it back on 66, and drove east. He accelerated up to speed slowly allowing time to enjoy the scenery. It reminded him of the scenery from Show Low to 66 that he had traveled through just a couple of days earlier.

How time flies, he thought. *Seems like it was weeks ago not just three days.* He started thinking about how much time they had manipulated on this journey and how it had changed his perspective. But, even with all the manipulation and movement, they still returned to their time. *What it would be like if "my time" no longer existed for me?* he thought. *I wonder if that is that's what LEAX's race is facing now dealing with the B'stri?*

Hunter finished his thoughts just as they pulled into the parking area at Hackberry.

Scott, admiring the classic 1957 Corvette in front of the store, remarked, "What a great visual link to the history of driving on Route 66."

They got out of the car, went into the old general store, and started looking at all the memorabilia from the history of Route 66. It was a 66 fanatic's paradise. Hunt went over to the counter and ordered three waters.

"This is just incredible," Scott commented as they were looking at the various signs, decals, postcards, car parts, photos, and books about Route 66 that were available for sale. The pictures on the walls showed various spots on the Route throughout history.

LEAX thought, *I wonder how many of my people have seen or will see these exact sites at the exact time these photos were taken?*

LEAX watched Scott look at each item. "There seems to be much history about this road."

"Yes," Scott replied, "I spent ten months listening to professors and reading books at school but in the three days we have been on this trip...journey, I mean... I have learned significantly more than I did during all of those months." Hunt brought over their waters and Scott pointed out pictures of the Grand Canyon Caverns. Suddenly, the old Star Trek theme wafted throughout the store.

"There's the call for Scott."

"How do you know?" LEAX asked.

Hunter laughed, "Because no one would have that music on their phone except a Trek junkie like Scott."

"Oh yeah?" Scott retorted. "Who are all the pictures of that you have on the walls in your office?" *Point and match to me on that round,* Scott thought.

"Hello."

"Hello, Scott," the voice on the phone greeted him. "This is Doc. I think we can do business."

"Great. Wait'll I get a pencil and paper, Doc. Now, go ahead."

"The site was accessible from a turn near MP90 about thirty miles east of Kingman. You should park there and start south along the dry creek bed that starts almost at the milepost marker. Go about two miles due south and you should see a BLM marker near a large prickly pear cactus. It's covered by vegetation so you might have to do a little searching."

"Hold on, Doc, I'm writing all this down. All right, continue."

"If you go about twenty feet northwest of the cactus, you should see what looks like a large, flat, orange-colored rock sitting by itself. That is where I found the wall... almost directly underneath it. I cleared about ten feet of it and it looked like there may have been more. It wasn't that long ago so the wall should still be partially visible."

"Thanks, Doc. I appreciate your sharing this information."

"Are you looking for something specific, Scott?"

"We're trying to confirm where Mercury was for some historical research."

'Are you working on a book?"

"Nah, that's your department, Doc."

"Let me know what you finally determine either way. I am working on an update to my book and I will be glad to give you credit if you can confirm that it is indeed Mercury."

"Will do, Doc. Thanks again. Bye. All right, guys, let's get going."

The three of them went outside and got in the car. Hunt started the engine and made a wide turn out on to the old road.

"What're we looking for, son?"

"We need to find mile post 90 on the south side of the road." Scott had a broad smile on his face.

"Why the smile?"

"I may be a published researcher for doc's next book if we can verify the existence of Mercury."

"Good for you," LEAX told Scott.

"Here's mile post 90." Within minutes, they found an area where they could park the car. Hunter parked away from the road. They looked out at the expanse of unbroken desert.

"Here we go again," Hunter sighed. They got out of the car and Scott got the canteens and shovels, and passed them out to everyone. They put the canteen belts on and walked across the road.

When they got to the other side, Scott looked at his notes. "Does anyone see a dry creek bed?"

LEAX pointed at a serpentine of fine sand that wound its way southward. "Is that it?"

Hunt followed it visually as far as he could see and then confirmed, "It sure looks like it."

"Ok, guys, we need to walk about two miles due south."

"Do we need a compass, Scott?"

"Already have it, Pop."

"Yo, LEAX," Hunter mimicked the current street language. "Are we close enough to the source to register on your Locator?" LEAX pulled out the Locator and activated it. There was no reaction.

"All right then, let's get started." They began walking along the dry creek bed. In about an hour, Scott looked up and pointed at the looming cactus.

"Wow, that's impressive even from a distance. You can see the thing from over a hundred yards away," Hunter commented.

"Yeah, and, when we get there, we have to find a very small, metal BLM survey marker," Scott reminded everyone.

LEAX asked Scott, "What's a BLM marker?" Scott described a marker for LEAX. They continued walking until they reached the cactus.

"Doc said it was under the cactus so we will have to work around it carefully lifting the cactus plates to see if the marker is there."

After walking around the cactus several times, they decided to take a break. They sat down in the shade of the plant and took a few healthy swigs of water.

Finally, LEAX broke the silence. "What do we do now?"

"Why don't you see if the device is more active now that we might be closer to the mapRock?" Hunt suggested.

LEAX pulled out the Locator and activated it. Even in the bright sunlight, it was possible to see the intensity and the frequency of the flashing.

Scott took out the compass, oriented the group to the northwest, and they all began walking the prescribed twenty feet. When Scott called out "here," everyone stopped and started looking around. It only took LEAX a couple of seconds to find a corner of an adobe block that was peeking through the sandy desert floor.

"Try it now," Hunter suggested. LEAX pulled out the Locator and activated it. The device was more active but had not gone steady state indicating the mapRock was definitely somewhere in the immediate area.

"Let's see if we can follow the adobe." They started digging around where they assumed the wall to be and exposed it. When they had gone about twelve feet and uncovered about five inches of wall height, they stopped for a break.

"Can you check it again, LEAX, to see if the site of the location could be narrowed down? Otherwise we could wind up unearthing the entire wall." LEAX activated the Locator and walked along the uncovered wall. It flashed unchanging along the entire wall segment.

"Doesn't seem to vary any along the wall," LEAX commented. Then, by accident, LEAX pointed the Locator to the west and the staccato picked up significantly.

"Look at this," he called to the others. Scott and Hunter walked over to where he was standing. As LEAX rotated the Locator away from the west, the intensity died down.

"It's out there, out yonder," Scott announced in his best western drawl. They started pacing off ground and watching and listening to the intensity levels of the Locator. It reached a crescendo at one point and then the intensity dropped off with the next step.

"Let's see if we can triangulate a common spot," Hunter suggested. For several minutes, LEAX paced back and forth while Scott and Hunter marked intensity grids on the ground. When they were done, the hot spot was isolated by a spider web of rocks and sticks.

"Go get the shovels, Scott."

He returned quickly and lay the shovels down in front of his dad.

Scott picked up one of the shovels and muttered, "Yeah, I know. The cute kid gets to do all the work." Scott dug until he had opened a hole about a foot deep.

He stopped, looked at the hole, wiped the sweat off his forehead, and suggested, "I think it's someone else's turn."

Hunter looked at Scott, got up, took Scott's shovel, and began digging. Scott found some shade and dropped down under it.

When Hunter's shovel hit something that sounded like wood, his first comment was "Uh oh."

The three of them looked at the bottom of the hole to see what Hunter had hit. It was dark brown and appeared to be slabs of dense wood lying side by side.

Remembering Havre, LEAX pleaded, "No more snakes, please."

They began cleaning dirt off the top of whatever was buried in the sand. When they finished, they had cleared away a four foot by eight foot wooden covering that looked like it could have been a door.

"LEAX, check the Locator and see if this is our destination." LEAX pointed the Locator and activated it. The lights were on continuously and very bright.

"Looks like home," Hunter announced. LEAX stored the Locator and began feeling around the edge of the cover. Hunter noticed that there were pegs imbedded in the four corners.

"Scott, bring me a shovel." Between the two of them, they were able to pry off one corner. Sand began filling in the void left exposed by lifting the cover.

"It looks like a big hole underneath," LEAX said. A damp, acrid, stinging smell came out of the hole. LEAX recoiled from the opening and moved away quickly. Within moments of uncovering the hole, LEAX began to develop a headache that blurred his vision. He began to sway unevenly.

"LEAX, are you all right?" Scott asked.

"I don't know," he responded and then fell to the ground. He lay there seemingly comatose except for his gulping huge quantities of air as if he had just come up from being underwater for too long. The two men went over to him to see what they could do.

"He looks bad, Dad." LEAX's breathing was becoming shallower. Then, there was no movement or signs of respiration.

Scott looked at his dad. "Is he dead?'

"I don't know."

"Look at his face. It's turning gray."

"Let's try CPR." Hunter suggested.

Then, without warning, LEAX began breathing hard again. Between gulps, he managed to say, "I'll be fine." Good to his word, LEAX's breathing stabilized and he was able to sit up and then stand up. His face was still ashen and drawn though, mute testimony to what his body had just been through.

"What happened?" they both asked.

"Scott, did you say that this site was named because of a mercury mine?"

"Yeah. There was a small mine that operated for a number of years but could never be made a success so they stopped operations."

"I believe that, if what we uncovered was the old mercury mine, we may have been exposed to methyl mercury, an extremely toxic and lethal compound formed where natural mercury exists. I think that is what that bad smell was."

"Then, if the mapRock is in that hole, you can't help us find it"

"No, Hunter, and neither can you or Scott."

"Why?"

"Methyl mercury is lethal to all living creatures."

"Why didn't it affect us like it did you?" Hunt asked.

"It affects different living things in different ways at different speeds."

"If we held our breath and were only in the mine for short periods of time, is there a possibility we might not be affected?" Scott asked.

"I don't know. Maybe. Maybe not. However, just remember, it can kill you."

"We can't quit now," Hunter told LEAX. "There has to be a way."

"Maybe, if we take the cover off completely and let the stuff air out, it won't be so bad."

"Good idea, Scott." Hunter and Scott walked over to the now partially uncovered hole, picked up the shovels, and began prying the remaining corners of the covering. Soon, the cover was off revealing a large hole.

Standing on the edge of the hole looking into the blackness, Scott spoke first, "Is that something white I see down at the bottom?"

"Sure looks like it."

LEAX, hearing the conversation, asked, "What do you see?" Scott turned to answer LEAX and, when he did, the movement of his feet caused the sand at the edge of the hole to give way sending him tumbling into the mine.

"Scott." Hunter yelled as he saw his son swallowed up by the darkness. He jumped in without regard for his own safety. The layers of dirt and sand that had filtered into the hole softened the impact of his fall.

"Scott, where are you? Are you all right?" Hunter was up on his feet quickly looking for his son. He found him over to the side, limbs motionless splayed out in all directions.

"Scott, wake up." Hunter shook Scott hard several times and then waited. Then Hunter realized the situation. *We're both in the mine possibly coming under the influence of the mercury. Am I going to be able to get Scott out of here in time?* He had no idea how they were going to get out or even if they could. He only knew that he had to try to bring his son back regardless of the cost to himself. "Scott," he called out again and shook his son. This time he heard Scott groan and saw some movement. While he was waiting for Scott to recover, he began looking around the mine. Several tunnels veered off the main room.

Where's that white object we saw?

Across the floor, he saw the white object. It was the remains of a human skeleton or what could pass as one. A tattered lab coat wrapped around the remains of the rib cage. The bone frame looked normal but the skull looked a little misshapen like the eye sockets were closer together. Then he saw that something metal was imbedded in the top of the skull.

What are these? he asked as he passed his fingers over the skull. *They look like bullet holes. I wonder how those got there?* The right hand or more precisely what was in the right hand caught Hunter's eyes. At that moment, Scott sat up.

Hunter turned his attention to his son. "How are you?" Scott looked at him and then around the floor.

"All I remember is slipping and falling and hitting my head on something hard."

"You took a pretty nasty fall when the lip of the opening caved in."

Scott looked up at the opening and then asked with some concern, "How did you get down here?"

"Ya know, I had to wait for this big lady to get off the dang escalator," Hunter remarked with a straight face. Then more seriously, "When I saw you fall, I jumped in after you." The look on Scott's face changed.

"What about the mercury stuff?"

"It doesn't seem to have impacted us."

"So far." Scott remarked.

Hunter turned his attention to the skeleton. He got up and went over to take the box out of its hand.

Scott saw where his dad was going and asked, "Who or what is that?"

"I don't know for sure but I have a strange feeling LEAX might know something about it."

"What's in the box?"

As he opened the box, Hunter replied, "I think it might be …yes, it is." The open box revealed a crystalline structure that looked exactly like…a mapRock. Hunter picked it up and turned it over in his hands. It was their mapRock. Suddenly, they heard LEAX.

"Are you two all right down there?"

"Yes, Scott and I are fine. I think we found the mapRock and something else rather interesting."

"What?"

"I'll have to show you." Hunter gave the box to Scott and started to look around for a way out. Because he had spent so much time in the company's Old Dominion mine, he had a better than average working knowledge of old mines. He knew that the room they were in was the anteroom for the miners.

The anteroom was the connection between the outside world and various underground mining operations. Because almost everyone who visited the mines started in the anteroom, they needed to have a convenient method of getting in and getting out.

Hunter looked around and found an old wooden entry and exit ladder.

"Scott, can you climb?"

"I think so."

"Let's get our butts outta here, then." Hunt picked up the skeleton and, when he did, he saw a small piece of paper under the rib cage. He grabbed it intending to look at it more closely once they got out of the mine. The fall didn't seem to affect Scott as he was up the ladder quickly.

About half way up, he stopped and began to read off a small, yellowing card on the wall. "Mining claim, Mercury, Arizona, 1875. This is Mercury for sure," he announced. He continued climbing and was out in a couple of minutes followed closely by Hunter with the skeleton. They went directly to where LEAX was and sat down.

LEAX stared at the skeleton for a time and then noticed the box. He opened it and looked at the mapRock.

"Was there anything else in it?"

"Nothing," Hunt replied.

Then LEAX put the box down and picked up the skull. He looked at the facial features and then at the occipital implant and what appeared to be bullet holes.

"Do you know what this is, LEAX?"

"I think so."

"It's an Oent'rfazr, isn't it?" Hunter declared.

'Yes." LEAX answered. "All of the early time traveling Oent'rfazr had a temporal transplant imbedded in their skulls at an early age. It performed a number of life support functions while the individual was in time travel status."

"Do you have one, LEAX?" Scott asked.

"No, they stopped implants when the technology changed."

"Anyway, what do you think happened, LEAX?" Hunter asked.

"It's likely that he was on his way to hide the mapRock for us to find when he, and this is the part subject to conjecture, materialized in the middle of the shoot-out. Before he could get out of the line of fire, he was hit twice in the head damaging the implant.

"So, he got caught in the crossfire, too?"

"Yes, unable to maintain his balance, he stumbled and probably fell into the mine. He likely survived long enough to try to hide the mapRock before either the mercury or the bullets finished him." Hunter remembered the piece of paper he found at the skeleton.

While Scott and LEAX were examining the skeleton further, he took the paper out of his pocket. *A pilot by Dr. Scott Johnson and Dr. Margaret Johnson.* Hunter realized it was talking about his wife and son. *Is this about their future that does not involve me in any way?* He put the paper back in his pocket for later as they prepared to leave. They sealed the old mine, covered the door, and buried the skeleton.

'Are you sure you're all right, LEAX?"

"I am fine now." They gathered everything up and walked back towards their car. As they were walking back to the car, Hunter called Scott over to his side.

"When I was lifting the skeleton out of the mine, I found this piece of paper under it. I picked it up to read it later. I thought you might want to see it." He handed the paper to Scott, who opened it and read it.

He looked at his dad. "What does this mean?"

"I think it means that sometime in the future you and mom will earn your doctoral degrees and work together on a major project."

"With you?"

Hunter hesitated. "I don't know. You saw the page. My name wasn't on it. Maybe it's a future that I am not part of. But, I thought you should know what is ahead for you and your mom."

Scott got very quiet.

As they got near the car, Scott put his arm around his dad's shoulder and said, "Thank you, Pop. You risked your own life for me by jumping in the mine not knowing if the mercury would kill you. You and I both are very lucky. You because nothing happened to you and me . . . because you're my dad."

Hunter just smiled and rubbed Scott's head.

Atomic Bombs

The trio drove west along the rolling hills and valleys that dotted the landscape with late Autumn colors. The drive felt peaceful after the events in Mercury.

Scott was on his phone. "Yeah, Doc, we did find the site and we did confirm that it was Mercury. You can put it in the 'it was right where I thought it was' section of your book."

Bright Route 66 shields painted in crisp, clean white paint on the surface of the asphalt created a 'follow me' trail into Kingman.

When Scott finished his call, he cleared his throat and announced in a loud voice, "You're now looking at the newest contributor to Doc Lee's *Newly Discovered Sites on Route 66.*"

"Is that the name of his next book?" Hunter asked.

"Yes, and I am going to be mentioned in it." Hunter gave him a thumb up and LEAX nodded his head.

"Ok, guys, we're looking for *Abomb* and Kingman is the next likely spot." In a few minutes, the roadway opened out into a long stretch leading to the outskirts of what looked like a small town.

"Is that an airstrip, Scott?" Hunter asked.

"Yup," Scott replied as he focused on the computer screen. "Kingman is the last large town on Route 66 before reaching the Arizona-California border. It's in the middle of a great high desert with only minimal access to water from the Colorado River located some hundred and fifty miles away."

"Gee, that reminds me. I'm thirsty," Hunter joked.

"One of the strangest things . . . if not the strangest thing . . . to happen in Kingman," Scott began, "was Project Genesis proposed by the federal government in the 1950s to cut waterways from the Colorado River eastward to create arable farmlands and navigation canals for northwest Arizona."

"That doesn't sound overly strange. I would think that would benefit everyone," Hunt commented.

"They planned to sculpt the canals to create the waterways by detonating twenty surplus atomic bombs left over from testing in New Mexico."

"Are you serious, Scott?" He nodded.

"They were already building the grandstands for the guests who were going to speak and then watch the detonations. Luckily, someone was smart enough to cancel the project before they could detonate any bombs. If they had completed the project, the entire corner of Arizona would have been uninhabitable for more than two hundred years, not to mention the deaths from radiation of all the people and animals that already lived there. This is all myth as no one could ever find proof of such a project. But it's a match for our next dream word."

"Sounds like our kind of place," LEAX commented uncharacteristically.

"Turn on Highway 27 and go north for approximately twenty-five miles, Dad." It was a dusty, unmarked, and unmaintained desert road that was not much more than a wide walking trail. They drove slowly through the open desert looking for any kind of remains. LEAX periodically activated the Locator to check for reactions as they got closer to the twenty-five mile limit.

"We must be getting close," LEAX commented as he watched the flashing slowly increase. They looked around the area but couldn't see anything but brush and rocks. Hunter stopped the car and they all got out. He took the binoculars out of the glove box and began scanning the desert taking time to look for areas that might display evidence of past human activity.

"Guys, I think I found something. Take a look." He handed the binoculars to LEAX and pointed toward the mountains. "Look at that fence."

"I see it."

"Do you see anything unusual about it, LEAX?"

"No, looks like a basic fence."

"Scott, take a look at the fence."

Scott took the binoculars and scanned the length of the fence.

"Interesting. It looks like a relatively new fence or one that has been very well maintained. And the sign that says Trespassers will be subject to deadly force without any previous warning is a sobering message." Scott handed the binoculars back to his dad. "Think that might be our destination?"

"If you have money, bet it all on that." Hunter looked around again. "I don't see a road leading to the fence. I guess that means we walk...again."

Scott grabbed the backpacks and gave them to the other two people. Then, he walked up behind LEAX and dropped a hat on his head. "You might need this."

LEAX reached up, lifted the hat off his head, turned it around feeling the material, and then put it back on his head adjusting it to a rakish angle to emulate Hunter and Scott. They all started walking toward the fence.

LEAX turned to Hunter. "What do you think we will find?"

"If this is the spot, it will probably depend on how much the government chose to leave behind. They're good at just walking off and leaving things where they fall."

"This is hotter than any other area we've walked in so far," Scott commented as they reached the fence.

"This is a pretty nice fence to be way out here in the desert. It must be here for some reason," Hunter told the guys. They crossed through the fence and sat down so that LEAX could check the Locator for a direction. It showed strong signals north of their location. "It looks like we need to follow this ridge," LEAX suggested.

"No time like the present," Hunter shot back.

They walked along the crest until they saw a series of what looked like foundations intermingled among large growths of cactus and desert sage.

"Might be something there," Scott remarked.

They carefully walked down the inclined side of the gorge working to keep their balance as the talus gave way under foot. They reached the bottom of the ridge and began walking towards the foundations.

"It looks like there were maybe a dozen buildings around here at one time. It's hard to tell what they were. Between nature and the folks who vacated the property, the area was effectively rendered unidentifiable. Very unusual for the feds."

They walked around each of the foundations. One had the remnants of a heavily traveled road leading up to it and then heading north. Hunter noticed Scott looking eastward at some smaller ridges.

"What're you looking at, Scott?"

"I thought I saw something sticking up out of the sand over there."

The three men gathered near one of the foundations while LEAX checked the Locator. It registered strongly.

"This looks like where we want to be," LEAX remarked. "Are you ready?"

"Wait, do we know what we're going to pop-up in the middle of? We better be ready in case we find ourselves in the middle of something that doesn't like us or wants us for breakfast," Hunter commented.

"What do you suggest?"

"I don't know. Just be ready to run or to transport back here quickly." LEAX confirmed he would be ready.

"Let's do it," Hunt replied.

Scott watched them disappear and then decided to explore the area away from the foundations, where he'd seen the object in the distance earlier.

Hunter and LEAX materialized in the middle of a large group of buildings.

"This looks a whole lot different now," LEAX exclaimed. The buildings were painted olive drab with a number of keep out and no trespassing signs. The door to the building they were standing next to had bright yellow signs with black triangles on them.

Hunter pointed at the signs. "Radioactive materials." Then he whispered quietly, "Look." The sign across the top of the doorway read: Atomic Storage Facility. Danger. Unauthorized Personnel Will Be Shot Without Warning.

"Warm invitation," Hunter acknowledged. Deep tracks in the sand were signs of recent heavy vehicle traffic around the building. Hunter heard the muffled sound of a truck engine coming their way.

"Hide," Hunter whispered and then pushed LEAX behind the building opposite the storage area. As they watched from the shadows, a small truck drove up next to the storage building and stopped. Two men got out of the front seat and moved quickly to the back of the truck where they flipped open a canvas covering.

"Ok, everybody out now," an older man in a uniform commanded in a low voice. Four soldiers quietly got out of the back of the vehicle. One of the men motioned for silence and pointed at the door to the storage facility.

"Let's get in, get the thing, and get out of here," the leader again commanded quietly. Just as he was opening the lock on the door, a squad of armed men came out from behind the buildings. The M-1's were aimed directly at the soldiers attempting entry.

"Halt. You're all under arrest."

One of the soldiers started to run. "Shoot him," the squad leader commanded. Several of the squad members trained their rifles on the retreating soldier. Multiple shots rang out. The fleeing solder slumped to the ground dead. Seeing that, the others dropped their weapons, put their hands up, and bunched into a group. The armed squad surrounded them and marched them away at gunpoint, leaving the dead soldier where he fell.

"I'm glad we caught these guys before they could steal another bomb," the squad leader told the soldier next to him. They fell into step behind their men.

Hunter looked around. "Let's find the mapRock and get outta here before we get the same treatment."

"What were the soldiers doing?" LEAX asked.

"It sounded like they were trying to steal an atomic bomb for some reason and they got caught. Atomic bombs were very dangerous so the army kept them under very tight security."

"Did I hear them say it was the second bomb?" LEAX questioned.

"Yes, but he didn't say what happened to the first one." LEAX started scanning the buildings and soon found one where the Locator showed the mapRock to be.

"It's in that building," LEAX told Hunter, "near that corner."

"We're not going to try to get into the building because of what would happen if we got caught. I'm sure it's wired. Should we be able to find it if we go back to our present?"

"Yes," LEAX answered. The two moved quickly together to touch the Locator and return to the present before they were discovered, or worse, before they were the cause of an atomic incident. They materialized among the desert growth and the foundations.

"Where's Scott?" Hunter asked.

They began looking for Scott but couldn't find him. After several minutes, LEAX told Hunter, "Look, here he comes."

His walk was unsteady and he staggered slightly from side to side as if he had a few too many.

Hunter called out, "Scott, is everything all right?"

Scott shook his head. "I think so."

"What happened?" LEAX asked.

"After you left, I went over to see what the thing was I saw when we arrived. It was a vent for an underground bunker almost covered by the desert. After I looked around a bit, I started to walk back here. Suddenly, the whole area went black. I felt like I was floating with no sensation of place, time, or physical existence."

LEAX's expression changed as Scott spoke.

"I was just conscious of the darkness, nothing else. I tried to feel for sensation in my body but there was nothing. I listened for a moment but couldn't hear anything. It was like I had been removed from my body."

The last part of the description caused LEAX to show fear in his face.

"I couldn't tell what had happened nor what time had passed but suddenly I felt a sensation like coming up out of a swimming pool. Then it was light and I was back walking toward you guys."

Hunt asked, "How do you feel now?"

Scott replied, "I am all right. Did you locate the mapRock?"

"We were just getting ready to look for it." Hunter and LEAX walked over to the corner of the building and began scanning with the Locator. They found the spot and began digging under the corner of the concrete. Within minutes, they located the box. LEAX pulled the mapRock out and called to Hunter. "Can you hold on to this for me?"

LEAX started to walk forward and, as he did, Scott moved and stumbled into him, knocking him down. When he fell, the mapRock dropped out of his hands. The sound of shattering glass was unmistakable.

LEAX reacted with a loud, "No." He studied Scott intently for a moment.

Scott just stared at the shattered mapRock. "I can't believe I just broke it."

LEAX stood up and motioned to Scott and Hunter to come over to him.

"We must be very careful from now on. The B'stri has been at various locations where we were and in various forms. He has been present when we were not aware of him. I think we just saw an example of his treachery and cunning."

"What're you saying?"

"Remember, I told you that the B'stri could for a time assume the physical identity of another person, while leaving the person in a kind of suspended animation? Based on what Scott described happened to him, I think he was in that suspended animation."

"Are you saying that wasn't Scott?"

"Yes. Now that he has come out in the open like this, it's a sign that he's more dangerous than ever. We need to watch for any unique behaviors among ourselves, in case he tries again through one of us."

"What can we do now about the mapRock?" Hunt asked.

"Nothing we can do now except try to find the technology using the remaining word clues because the mapRocks won't work."

"Isn't there something we can substitute?" Scott queried.

"Nothing. It has to be the mapRock designed for this circuit."

"I guess that wraps it up for us here then," Hunter sighed.

"No," Scott replied. "There has to be another way."

"I don't think so," LEAX said.

Frustrated, they sat down to try to figure out what their next step was before returning to Kingman. Scott was desperately trying to figure out something.

"Wait," he yelled. "Can you go back to the same site earlier than the first time you were there?"

"Yes, we can."

"I want to go back now," Scott growled. "Right now."

"I suppose you could but why would you want to?"

"Just take me back to the site now, LEAX." Scott showed he was in no mood to discuss his request.

LEAX looked at Hunter who nodded his concurrence.

"I am not sure exactly how it will work so soon before the first visit. It could be dangerous."

"I don't care. Let's go *now.*"

"Okay," LEAX replied, not sure how to react to this new side of Scott.

LEAX and Scott made the connection with the Translator and they disappeared leaving behind a very worried Hunter. When they materialized in the past, LEAX took the detector out of his belt and started following Scott.

"LEAX, where did you find the MapRock?" Scott asked. Just at that moment, a soldier walked around the corner and surprised them. LEAX and Scott froze while the soldier immediately pulled out his sidearm and commanded, "Halt. Don't move or I'll shoot."

The three stood there facing one another. Just as the soldier was ready to speak, an obscene screeching sound that hurt the eardrums pierced the air. The soldier looked around as if trying to make a decision.

"Get inside the building, now," he ordered LEAX and Scott. They moved slowly until the soldier shoved them against one another and into the side of the building. The soldier unlocked the door, pushed them roughly inside, and then locked the door.

"I'll be back for you later," he told them and then sprinted away as fast as he could.

Scott and Hunter were confined in a small office with a number of desks, chairs, and file cabinets. Scott sat on one of the desks. He noticed a single folder that was marked in large red letters: TOP SECRET: BASE COMMANDER EYES ONLY.

"Maybe we lucked out and this is the right location. LEAX, see if you can find the mapRock." Scott opened the folder and began reading while LEAX started checking the doors and windows for a possible way out. Finding none, he started checking the floor area to see if this was the building where they found the mapRock.

"Scott, it's in this corner."

Scott absent-mindedly put the paper in his pocket and told LEAX, "Let's get out of here, find the mapRock, relocate it, and get back to my dad."

"Everything is locked," LEAX commented. Scott grabbed a large paperweight and broke the window. After removing the glass, they were able to open the window and crawl out and to locate the mapRock. Scott hurried to the bunker he had explored while waiting for LEAX and Hunter to return and then lodged the mapRock at the bottom of the air vent. He returned to where LEAX was, touched the Transporter with him, and they were back in the present.

"What happened? Hunter's concern was obvious.

"I figured that we might be able to go back and change the location of the mapRock. The first version of the mapRock that you found was broken but the version in the past should still be intact. If I am right, we should find the new unbroken pre-version of the broken mapRock where I put it."

"What a great idea, Scott. I hope it works."

The three of them walked to the bunker where Scott bent down and opened the air intake. He reached in, pulled out the now familiar mapRock, and handed it to LEAX.

"Now, all we have to do is see if it will work in the loop," LEAX said. "Unfortunately, we won't be able to tell that until we have all of them."

LEAX put the mapRock in his belt and helped the guys gather up the items they brought from the car. Then they walked back to their car.

"Let's get all this stuff loaded and get on the road," Hunter suggested. The three finished loading the trunk and got into the car. There was a feeling of renewed optimism as they drove southward.

Scott remembered the letter he took from the base. He took it out of his shirt.

"Listen to this, guys. Approximately two weeks ago, an atomic device was stolen off the Kingman base. It was one of twenty stored atomic bombs to be used for Project Genesis north of Kingman. A plot by one of our enemies with the help of some traitors from within was to take the bomb to Hoover Dam, park it overnight, and then detonate it thereby destroying the dam and flooding the Colorado River and the areas it serves with intense radioactivity."

Hunter turned around. "Why did they want to do that?"

Scott continued reading. "This would destroy all of southern California and the entire western half of Arizona not to mention Mexico and its seaports. The economic and military response capability of the US would be reduced by over 30%, rendering it susceptible to economic and military subjugation."

Hunter was curious. "Where did you get that? That document proves the existence of the Genesis Project."

"It was in a folder on top of one of the desks in the area where we were held. But wait, there's more to the whole Genesis story. On the way to the dam, the truck transporting the bomb was rerouted because of an accident and had to detour along the edge of Lake Mead. The driver misread a corner and the back end of the trailer slid off the road and the bomb rolled into the lake somewhere northeast of the dam."

Hunter asked, "Did they recover it?"

"At this time, the bomb is still in the lake possibly damaged, possibly leaking radiation, and, because of the impact with the lake bottom, possibly armed."

"We were at the base two separate times and saw two different scenarios," LEAX reminded them. "What caused those?"

"Put the base on 'Red 1' security as Washington believes that there may be an attempt to steal a second bomb. Shoot to kill anyone you cannot identify on sight even if they are wearing one of our uniforms. That's it." Scott folded the letter and put it away.

"Wow," Hunter reflected, "that is one that will never be in the history books. I wonder if they ever found the bomb or if they wrote it off and it's still there today?"

"Wherever it is, I hope it is still resting quietly," Scott commented.

"If it decides to make itself known, I guess we won't really have anything to say about it," Hunter replied, "or even know that it went off."

The car was quiet and then Scott suggested, "We can bypass Kingman and pick up 66 by turning right at the junction of 44."

"Thanks. And, by the way, I am very proud of you, Scott. You showed some incredible initiative, critical thinking ability, ingenuity, and just plain guts based on what you did back there. For your first time travel, anything could have happened. Going back to get an earlier copy after the first mapRock got broken was pure genius."

LEAX turned his right hand palm up and put it on top of his left hand. Scott just smiled.

UFO Cave

The three men began the drive south from Kingman on the way to connect with the last leg of Route 66 before the California line. Soon, the caverns, the Mercury mine, and the mapRock issue at the atomic base began to have their collective effects on all three men. The car was inundated with yawns and stretching.

Scott thought for a moment. "LEAX, is there an equivalent to what we call jet lag for time travelers?"

"Jet lag?"

"When a person changes time zones frequently on long trips, his body gets out of sync with the world around him and he gets very sluggish and sleepy because he's awake when he should be sleeping and vice versa."

LEAX thought for a moment. "I guess there is. That may be why we're all reacting now."

"What's the best way to deal with it?"

"Rest, like any other tiredness."

"How about we make this day a short one then, camp out, and get some solid rest for tomorrow?"

Hunter looked at LEAX. "Sounds good to me."

"You remember what we talked about in the cavern," LEAX reminded Hunter. "Delaying may result in failure or worse."

"We definitely need to rest in case we have to be able to think and react on critical decisions later on." Hunter started looking for a good camping spot. Just as he drove past Connico, a once thriving stop for 66 travelers, there was a sign that read: Kingman UFO Cave Campground two miles.

"Let's give it a shot." He turned the car south and headed into the Hualapai Mountains. The road was dusty but showed signs of recent maintenance. Within minutes, they were driving into an open area surrounded by mountains on three sides. The sign said: Campsites are free just keep them clean.

They found a quiet site with a great view of the camp, the mountains, and the sky. Hunter pulled in and parked the car. Scott looked at the sign for this campsite.

"Look how large those numbers are. No one could miss those even with their eyes closed," Scott reminded his dad of what happened at the crater. The three men unloaded the gear and set-up the camp. Having LEAX help cut the set-up time considerably.

"Scott, how about cooking one of your specialties tonight?"

"Ok, Pop, you got it. But, before it gets too dark, can we walk around the area. It will be nice to just look at scenery to enjoy it and not be trying to figure out if and where a mapRock might be hidden."

"I agree, Scott," Hunter answered. LEAX was looking around the immediate area checking out large clumps of bushes, crevices in the mountainside, and camping neighbors.

Scott looked at Hunter who mouthed the word, *B'stri*.

Scott nodded and put a jacket on for their walk. Just as they were getting ready to leave, a woman in a green uniform walked into camp.

"Hello. My name is Samantha. I'm the host ranger here at the campsite." The three introduced themselves.

"Where are you from?" she looked to Hunter.

"Globe. Up here being tourists. Been traveling the northern part of the state," Hunter replied cautiously.

"It's nice up here this time of year but not very many people come out an enjoy it," Samantha said.

Scott jumped into the conversation. "I'm a student at NAU and we do a lot traveling in this part of the state but I don't recall seeing this camping area listed anywhere. Is it new?"

"Yes, it's only been open a couple of weeks."

"Quite a unique name. Is there a story behind it?" Hunter was looking for additional information that might prove helpful.

"Yes. About eighteen months ago, the town tore down some dilapidated buildings that had become a safety hazard, including one that had reputation of being used by extraterrestrials. The workers came across some notes that mentioned several locations in Arizona where non-humans appeared with some regularity… including this area."

Scott commented, "I think NAU is probably one of those locations based on the appearance and behavior of some of the kids and professors in my classes."

Samantha chuckled and continued. "In May 1953, it was reported that a saucer shaped craft crashed in this general area. Supposedly, a busload of scientists and military people came here in a bus and saw the downed craft with a large hole in the side and four small body bags with bodies in them lying on the ground. The bus took the people away in about an hour and no one has been able to identify whom they were or where they went. The story is that they had the UFO and body bags taken to that deserted building in downtown Kingman."

"Has anything happened there recently?" LEAX inquired.

"Nothing."

"Where is the cave?" Scott asked.

"That the other strange thing. People who used to hike out here swore there was a cave just a bit east of here but no one has been able to find any evidence of it."

"So no one has found anything-UFOs, bodies, notes, people on a bus, or caves?"

"Kingman officials thought it would be a great attraction to tie all the stories to a site in the mountains."

"Can you show us where all this 'supposedly' took place?" LEAX posed the question Scott was getting ready to ask.

"Sure. Grab your coffee. It's only about a five minute walk from here." The four people walked out of camp and followed a rustically marked trail. It ended in a small open area posted with two signs. One told the story of the saucer that crashed right where the sign was and the other told the story about the missing cave.

Samantha laughed. "The PR department knows just how much baloney to put out there so they can get the people to at least wonder if the events are true." They walked around a bit more and then decided to return to camp.

"Samantha, would you like to come over for dinner?" Hunter suggested.

"No. Thank you. I have a bunch of paper work to do but I might drop over for some coffee later."

The people went back to camp and Scott started the campfire to cook dinner.

Hunter looked thoughtful. "LEAX, any chance some of your people ...our people... might have been the source of those rumors and stories?"

"I wondered that, too," Scotty added.

"Anything is possible," LEAX replied. "That reminds me. What is our next word, Scott?"

Scott put his spatula down and opened his list. "*Numbers.*"

Scotty put the stew ingredients in the pot and began cooking it. "Dad, where's the Irish flavoring?" Hunt got up, went to the trunk of the car, and came back with a small bottle of brown liquid. He gave it to Scott who poured about half of it into the stew and stirred it.

"I think you'll like this special stew, LEAX," Scott said winking at his dad. It was rapidly getting dark and there was no moon but there was a sky full of beautiful stars. The three men ate their stew slowly and talked about the last three days.

"I could probably write a book about all the strange experiences we've had on this trip and I don't just mean the traveling in time. I am still shaking from what we saw and heard in the caverns and at Two Guns," Hunter shared.

"It's not unusual for there to be many unexplained occurrences when we travel. There are some of my people who think that when we time travel a link or doorway opens simultaneously to another world that involves other pasts or possibly other futures."

The blanket of evening quiet covered the three men. The orange glow of the campfire highlighted the effects of the last three days on the faces of the travelers. A lone coyote howled in the distance breaking the silence. The three of them had been talking for nearly three hours.

"We should probably hit the sack" Hunter told everyone. "After all, that is why we made this stop."

LEAX got up to go get a final cup of coffee and he banged into the camp table. Suddenly, the locator lit up. It stayed lit for a time and then went dark.

I wonder what caused that? LEAX thought. *Maybe hitting the table caused a temporary connection of some kind?*

No one noticed that when the Locator went dark a mild wind began to blow, almost imperceptibly, through the camp.

The guys cleaned up the campsite, put out the campfire, and headed into their tents. The wind had continued to pick up strength slowly so that now it was more obvious. Within a short time, the sounds of sleep echoed through the camp. The wind continued quietly until around two when it turned destructive and noisy. As it became stronger, it knocked over tables and chairs and woke the three men.

"What the hell is going on out there?" Hunter almost yelled. They came outside their tents and began looking around. Scott was the first to notice.

"There's a weird glow coming from the area we were at tonight." They looked toward the site where the saucer was supposed to have crashed and it was actually glowing. "Now what's going on over there?" Hunt emphasized the now. They grabbed flashlights and, as they ran over to the area, they had to work to keep from being knocked over by the wind. When they entered the area, they saw the rock face where the cave was supposed to have been flashing like someone was turning a light off and on.

LEAX scanned the face of the rock with the Locator and, when he did, the wind died down and the alternating flashes stopped. The rock face was dark momentarily and then a series of small light flashes moved around randomly on the face. They began to morph into numbers and Scott read them off as they appeared.

"33, 39, 443" and then they stopped. Scott looked at his dad and then the flashing began again. This time the numbers were different.

"-114, 39, 598."

The flashing stopped and the area returned to darkness. The air got very still. There was no noise or wind and the stars twinkled brighter than Scott ever remembered seeing them. The three men walked slowly back to camp talking about what had just happened. They straightened the camp furniture and lights and sat down. Scott wrote the numbers down.

"That was unbelievable. Do you think it had something to do with our journey even though there was no mapRock involved?"

"Unsure," LEAX responded.

"What do you think the numbers meant?" Hunter asked. "It was interesting how they appeared in groups. Scott, did you get the spacing with the numbers?" Scott nodded.

They went back to their tents and tried to go back to sleep. All three slept fitfully.

Hunter was up early making coffee, as usual.

When Scott came out of his tent, Hunt questioned him. "Did you happen to see what time it was when we went out last night?"

"It was around two o'clock, I think,"

I wonder if it was 2:20? Hunt thought. At about that time, Samantha came walking into camp.

"Good morning, everybody."

"Good morning," Hunter replied.

"Sorry I didn't make it over for coffee last night. I started on that paperwork and then I fell asleep and heard nothing until about an hour ago. It was as if someone drugged me. Never had that happen before."

"You didn't hear the wind that tore through this place or see the lights?" Hunter inquired.

Samantha looked strangely at the three of them. "Wind? Lights? I didn't hear or see anything."

"Maybe it was a result of hearing the stories about the aliens and the UFOs," Hunter feigned a smile.

"Where are you guys headed today?"

"We really aren't sure. Just being tourists. Would you like some coffee, Samantha?"

"I would love it." Hunter poured a cup and handed it to her.

"This is a great place," LEAX told her. "I hope more people find out about it."

"Me too, she replied. She started talking about what it was like in the campgrounds while she finished her coffee. When she was done, she said "Thanks" and headed back to her office.

Hunter started putting stuff in the trunk. He put part of the gear down by the sign that designated the number of the site and then stopped in his tracks.

"LEAX. Scott. Come here."

The two came running to where Hunter was.

"Look at this," Hunt exclaimed pointing at the sign. "The Oent'rfazr symbol. Was it there when we came in yesterday?"

"No," Scott said. "I looked very closely at the sign when we came in."

LEAX looked perplexed. "We may have had an Oent'rfazr visitor last night, which is why we were awakened and then shown those numbers."

"Does it usually happen like that?" Scott looked at LEAX.

"No, that was totally out of the ordinary… just like a number of things have been on this journey," LEAX said with some finality.

"Could it have been the B'stri?"

"I don't think so. Because of the potential power of the symbol, only a few Oent'rfazr have access to its use. If it was the B'stri, it could mean something very bad is happening in my world."

Hunter watched LEAX as they finished packing the car. The expression on his face never changed.

Oatman

Their car, covered with the dust from the windstorm at the campsite last night, was soon back on the highway headed south. Savoring his successful first travel effort in Kingman to save the mapRock, Scott looked quite pleased with himself.

"Guys, the next words are *numbers* and then *oatie*. We didn't find any mapRock where we found the numbers at the campsite but, based on the sign up ahead, it certainly seems that *oatie* is the more appropriate choice of the two."

LEAX commented, "If the numbers were a message, which it appears they are, then the Oent'rfazr could have left the word *numbers* to tell us to check for different sites on the journey."

"Are you saying that *oatie* might indeed be the next word?"

"Yes."

Hunter noticed the road sign they were talking about that read: Oatman thirteen miles. "Think there might be a connection?"

"Let's go find out" LEAX told Hunt.

Hunt turned the car west along Old Route 66. They passed several old foundations where buildings once existed when the Route was the only way from Kingman to the California border.

Hunter looked at them. *More history gone.*

After passing the newly rebuilt Cool Springs store, they began their climb up the Black Mountains. Scott and LEAX were enjoying the scenery when, as they topped out at Sitgreaves Pass, the unlinked mapRocks exploded in a ten second display of brilliant, multi-hued colors.

"What the heck is going on?"

"I've never seen an unlinked group of mapRocks do that before," LEAX said. "I'm not sure what could have caused it."

Scott interrupted. "Goldroad, the old ghost town, is just on the other side of the pass. Do you think that it could mean that the mapRock is there?"

"The mapRocks are not supposed to activate in any way until they're linked into a completed circuit and near the object that is being sought," LEAX repeated.

As the car began the descent, Hunt could see a series of long, sharp switchbacks that ended near what looked like an abandoned town at the bottom of the hill.

"There are just some old foundations, a part of a miner's wooden shack, old rusty machinery, and a partially sealed entrance to the main mine. Oh yeah, and a graveyard."

"We better stop and check it out, just to be sure," LEAX confirmed.

Hunt pulled the car over to the side of the road at the bottom of the switchbacks and they got out. LEAX picked up the Locator and started walking into the desert. Hunter stopped him.

"The town cemetery is in the direction you're heading. Be careful."

After about fifteen minutes, LEAX stopped at what he assumed was the graveyard. He deactivated and then re-activated the Locator several times but it still showed no reaction. He paused a moment to study the plot of land surrounded by a row of rocks and the remains of several wooden markers

"Any luck, LEAX?" Hunter called out.

"Nothing," LEAX responded and then walked back to the car in a semicircle checking to make sure he didn't miss any signs. He even ventured over to the mine opening but the results were still the same.

Hunt and Scott saw LEAX back at the car and hurried to meet him.

"Based on the Locator, the mapRock was never here," he told them.

"Then, let's get on to Oatman," Hunter suggested.

They got into the car and Hunt pulled back out onto the dirt road and began driving west towards Oatman. As he skillfully navigated the car around blind corners just wide enough for one car, Hunt glanced at LEAX, who was frowning while holding the box of mapRocks.

"I wish I knew what cause that reaction? I hope there isn't a malfunction with the mapRocks. That could damage our efforts right here."

Hunt turned the car around a blind corner and slammed on the brakes to keep from hitting an oncoming car.

When the car had passed, he commented to no one in particular, "I don't know how the drivers survived back then."

They drove around another sweeping, dusty curve and found themselves just outside the town of Oatman. It looked like many of the old towns they had seen along the journey except here dozens of cars were parked in front of the buildings and a throng of people was feeding the free roaming burros.

LEAX noted that the Locator was blinking. "It looks like we might have a possibility here. Now, we have to figure out what significant happened here. Scott, that's your cue."

"I'm on it. A small commercialized ghost town near the Arizona-California border on Route 66, Oatman is situated in the middle of the People's Mine, the most productive gold mine in the history of Arizona. Oatie is the resident ghost, who frequents the Oatman Hotel and talks to tourist in the wee hours of the morning."

"Sounds like that might be our man…er…ghost," Hunt suggested.

"When he was alive, he was a miner named Ray Flour, who emigrated from Ireland. The night before he was to leave for Washington to testify before Congress, a member of a local gang got him drunk, walked him out to the mines, and shoved him down into one. He was missing for several days but the townspeople refused to go looking for him so his body was never buried or even found."

"I bet that has something to do with why he's still around," Hunt added.

Scott looked at his dad. "It was about that time that Oatie began appearing at the hotel. Story has it that the ghost told the hotel owner that until they recovered his body and gave him a proper burial, he would continue to haunt the hotel."

"We probably should find the People's Mine and see if we get any reaction there," LEAX suggested. The three of them got out of the car and went into the Oatman Hotel. "Do you know where the People's Mine is?" Hunter posed the question to the desk clerk.

"It's behind the Elephant's Tooth." LEAX looked at Hunter and started to ask, but Hunt stopped him.

"It isn't a real elephant's tooth, LEAX. In the early west, people identified locations by what they resembled or what was special at the site."

The desk clerk, overhearing the conversation, pointed north of town, and commented with a bemused smile, "You can't miss it."

Hunter motioned to the other two. "Let's head north." They walked the short distance to the north end of town and looked into the mountains.

"There it is," Scott exclaimed, pointing at a very large rock formation that looked exactly like a large tusk. LEAX made sure he had the Locator and the Translator, in case they found evidence of the mapRock.

They locked the car and walked to the Tooth.

"It's going to be difficult to do our thing with so many people around," Scott commented as they walked through groups of tourists. The dusty trail wound around the various small rock formations creating the effect of doubling back on itself, but, in a short time, they reached an open area where they saw the sign for the People's Mine.

"Over there." Scott pointed at a small mine entrance. It'd been closed off to the public with crisscrossed rebar leaving openings small enough to look through but not small enough to get through. The three used the time to check quietly for mapRock readings.

"It doesn't look like it's here."

The three stared at one another for a few moments and then Hunter said, "I have a couple of thoughts." They found a small concrete picnic table and sat down. "Our word is *oatie*. Scott gave us a good description and we know where he isn't so now we need to go back to town and talk to people about him. Scott, you need to do some more Oatie searching on your laptop. We will meet at the hotel in two hours."

Scott found a wi-fi location in a small store and set-up his computer. LEAX and Hunter went through a number of stores along the main road. Scott finished reviewing more details on Oatie's life and packed up his computer to go to the hotel. As he crossed the creaking, wooden porch, he saw Hunter and LEAX walking and talking in a highly animated manner heading towards the hotel. He began walking their direction.

Hunter acknowledged Scott. "Did you find anything?"

"I did find some interesting things but I don't know if they will help us." The three made their way into the hotel coffee shop and took over a table in the corner.

"Ok, what dya have, Scott?"

"Ray left his wife and family in Ireland to seek his fortune in America. He did some extensive prospecting in northern Arizona finally settling in Oatman and staking several claims. He got very rich and sent money to his family to join him in America."

"What happened to them?" LEAX asked.

"They booked passage and were on their way to America when disaster struck. His wife and two kids were drowned when the Titanic hit the iceberg and sank. He never fully recovered and became a destructive alcoholic. He wondered around aimlessly until he died or, depending on whose story you follow, was murdered in the mine."

Hunter continued after Scott. "After he learned that his family had been lost, he staked out part of one of his claims and turned it into a pseudo graveyard for his family. The town folk said he even had headstones made for each family member."

"Another strange story, among many," Scott commented.

"He told everyone that he knew there would never be any bodies in the graves but they would help him accept what had happened."

"He must have really loved his family," Scott remarked.

"That isn't all," LEAX continued. "After Flour's body was lost and the town couldn't find him to bury him, they decided to make another symbolic grave for him next to his wife and family, in hopes that would appease Oatie."

"Somewhere out there is a graveyard with headstones, graves, but no bodies? Scott turned a statement into a question.

"Yes, and Flour's empty grave just might be our last hope. All we have to do now is find the grave sites."

"Is his claim marked in any way?" Scott inquired.

"We were told the claim was near a place that used to exist five miles west of Oatman called Riverview Court. They said the only things that would be on the claim now are part of an adobe foundation, a decaying wooden shack where Flour lived, some rusting mining gear, and the headstones."

The three men paid their tab and got in the car. They drove west until they found the clearing and what was left of a foundation. Hunter parked the car and they got out. There was no sign of any human habitation, other than the foundation, as far as they could see.

"I guess there is just one thing to do now," LEAX commented as he grabbed the Translator. This time all three men touched it. Where they materialized didn't look much different from the place they left. LEAX activated the Locator and scanned the horizon. There was a strong signal to the northwest. They grabbed a couple of shovels and started walking. They came to a small canyon that lead up into the mountains.

"There's his cabin," Scott called out as he pointed to a single brown structure partially hidden by the vegetation. They walked over to the cabin. The front door that swung back and forth in the wind on one hinge and the broken window glass identified the cabin had been abandoned.

"Let's check around the cabin." LEAX turned the locator on and it lit brightly.

The three men worked in a circle around the cabin.

Hunter yelled, "Here it is." They all gathered with Hunt. Scott read the headstones and the dates but didn't see any notation for Ray. They looked around but didn't find anything.

"We may have arrived before Ray's headstone was added. Now that we have the location of the graveyard, we can go back to the present, locate the graveyard, and see if Flour's headstone is there." Everyone agreed and they transported back.

Weeds, desert sage, and tumbleweeds choked the land. If they had not known the graveyard was there, they probably would've missed it.

"Any luck, Scott?" Hunt was hoping to hear a yes.

"Not so far," he replied as he began removing brush and found all three headstones in various conditions of decay. Over to one side, he discovered a large flat rock that he didn't remember seeing before. He turned it over and read the name Ray Flours hand printed in red paint. "I think I found him," Scott yelled.

LEAX pointed the Locator and the light was continuous. They dug down until they hit something solid.

"Seems like all we do is walk and dig," Hunter commented. "I should have enough experience credits for a degree in shoveling," he joked. Scott just stared at him but didn't say what he was thinking. Scott dug the object out the rest of the way by hand and handed it to LEAX. LEAX opened the box and removed the bag it contained. He opened the bag carefully, removed the mapRock, and handed it to Scott. Scott gasped.

"It's black. It's the last one."

LEAX looked at the ebon mapRock and, with some finality, announced, "Our journey is almost over." Hunter and Scott paused to let the gravity of LEAX's statement sink in.

Scott remarked, "I wonder if there's any significance that the mapRock that will complete the chain and perhaps initiate the action that will change the world as we know it, is black?" Scott stared at the mapRock. "I can't believe we're done."

LEAX turned around. "We are not done yet by any means."

A piece of paper that was in the mapRock box fell to the ground. Scott picked it up and quickly read the headline and the first sentence. "Johnson first to the future again. Three years ago, Dr. Hunter Johnson was the first human to astral project into the future." Then Scott stopped.

Goldfish Confrontation

"Now comes the difficult part," LEAX told Hunter and Scott. "Finding the technology." They walked back to the car and got in. Hunter started the car, LEAX grabbed the container of mapRocks, and Scott added the final mapRock to the collection. He was anxious to watch the linking process.

"How do you get this going?" Scott questioned LEAX.

LEAX answered, "I've never done this with real mapRocks by myself but it's a matter of plugging them into one another one at a time until we get a match."

"So, it's an electronic guessing game?" Scott suggested.

Scott watched LEAX. The instantaneous yes or no confirmation that resulted each time a link was attempted reduced the number of potential connection tries from over four million to a mere one hundred and eleven.

"Thank goodness for Oent'fazr technology," Scott mumbled. The first few connections were very slow because there were a large number to try but the speed increased as more connections were made.

"Scott, would you like to try the assembly?"

"Absolutely." Scott's emphatic yes echoed throughout the car. He was a little apprehensive about the mapRock that was shattered in Kingman. He still had a hard time wrapping his mind around the idea that something could be destroyed and still be whole.

"Done in less than twenty minutes," Scott announced. Their technology detector was operational. *One step closer to the end,* Scott thought.

"Now that we have all the mapRocks and they're connected properly, what next?" Hunter asked.

LEAX began, "Now we begin traveling to see if the linked circuit of mapRocks lights up anywhere along the way. Much like the Locator, the mapRocks will shine brighter the closer we get to the technology."

"Do you mean that now we just drive around now until that mapRock circuit lights up?"

LEAX nodded.

"That could take forever."

"Wait," Scott said. "There are still words left on the list." He checked for the next word and pronounced it to himself as if he wasn't sure what he was reading. Then, he said, "*Goldfish.*"

"Now, where are we going to find goldfish in water in the desert?"

"It doesn't say anything about water, Pop. It could be a dead goldfish, a picture, or a symbol of some kind." They drove through Oatman and were on their way back to Goldfield when Scott remembered.

"Hey, guys, remember what happened when we drove over Sitgreaves Pass this morning? Maybe we should start there."

"It's as good a place as any to start," LEAX agreed.

Hunt continued driving. They danced with the switchbacks up the side of the mountain much as a woman would follow a dance partner. As they neared the top, the link of mapRocks began to glow. Within minutes, they were at the top of the pass and parking the car.

"Let's see if we can find anything that indicates a historical event or some kind of location marker." They got out and started looking around. Hunt saw an old marker that named and described the pass. LEAX brought the mapRocks over but the intensity of the lights didn't change.

"Apparently, this isn't the spot." They searched the area but didn't find anything. They were standing together at the car talking when several tourists walked up the road and stopped near the group.

"Connor, that is the strangest thing I've ever seen," Cora said. "A fishbowl out in the middle of this desert with water and goldfish in it, no less. Just amazing."

"I know. I wonder how long it has been out there?" Connor replied.

Hunt interrupted. "Excuse me? Where did you see a fishbowl with goldfish?"

Connor pointed down the road. "About a tenth of a mile down there on the right at the top of some natural steps cut into the mountainside."

Hunter turned to Scott, "*Goldfish?*"

LEAX, Hunter, and Scott grabbed the mapRock chain and started walking towards the area that Connor described. As they approached the steps, the mapRocks didn't flicker; they burned steadily. They climbed the rock-hewn steps and found the fishbowl exactly as it was described. At the bottom of the fishbowl, there was an arrow with two heads pointing downwards. Other than the arrows, the three couldn't find any unusual markings.

"What if the arrows mean 'under the bowl'?" Hunter said to himself. He began digging unaware that LEAX was coming up behind him. Hunter continued digging at the base of the fishbowl and suddenly he hit something solid.

"Scott. LEAX." Hunter called out. He looked up to try to find Scotty and LEAX but didn't see them. He stood up and started to turn around to say something when LEAX stepped up behind him, swung his shovel in a wide arc, and smashed Hunter's face in one bone shattering crunch.

Scott yelled. "Dad."

The impact was so hard that Hunter dropped to the ground nearly unconscious, blood spilling out of his nose and mouth.

LEAX said, in a deep, crackly monotone voice that did not sound like the LEAX they had known, "Fools that you are. Now, I have the technology and, Hunter, you and your family are going to die." Scott started to move towards LEAX, but stopped as his dad started groaning and trying to sit up.

"Who are you?" Hunt's voice sounded weak, as he swayed unsteadily, trying to focus.

"I am one with the B'stri, who sent me to make sure you didn't find the technology."

"You acted like our friend," Scott yelled, grabbing ahold of his father to help him up.

"A clever trick to make sure that I found the technology before you."

"I don't understand?" Hunter managed to whisper through the pain.

"My people determined that your family would be the cause of the future destruction of the B'Stri and that we needed to prevent you from gaining access to the technology even if many of us had to die. But now, it will be simple matter to dispose of you and your family without a loss of B'stri life."

"At least, my wife will be safe."

"You are so simple-minded. I called her and told her to drive here as soon as possible. I will dispose of you and your son now and your wife in a few hours. The continued existence of the B'stri will be ensured," LEAX exclaimed. LEAX turned and finished digging out the box that contained the technology. He glanced at Hunter several times to make sure he was still down. He held up the box and looked for a way to open it.

That gave Hunter enough time to stagger to his feet and then whisper to Scott, "When I say now, shove me towards LEAX as hard as you possibly can."

"Dad—," Scott started to object.

"Just do it." LEAX opened the lid to the box and reached for the contents.

"Now." Scott slung his dad forward uncontrollably. Just as LEAX's hand touched the technology, Hunter's body slammed into him and Hunter touched the technology at the same instant.

LEAX shouted. "No."

Instantly, both men were enshrouded in a cocoon of red and blue light. At first, their bodies were highlighted by the dichromatic glow but then they began to blur into the colors and into each other, and then the two formless beings completely dissolved and imploded.

LEAX and Hunt were gone.

"Dad." Scott yelled as the compression wave from the implosion picked him up and slammed him backwards into a nearby hill. He lay motionless as he tried to catch his breath.

Scott tried to move his shoulders and back. *I feel like I was slammed with a huge baseball bat.* He got up slowly and looked around. He felt pain in his back but managed to move relatively quickly. He began walking towards the fishbowl where he had last seen his dad. He was the only living thing anywhere in sight. His boots created a ghostly sound as he walked through the gravel around the fishbowl.

It's like absolutely nothing happened here.

Aftermath

The technology lay on the ground in front of the fishbowl, a silent dedication to where the two men last touched and where they shared their last breath. Scott stopped and picked it up.

Is this what the last five days were all about? It must be something incredible considering what it cost our family. He stood there in stunned silence as if waiting for someone to appear or to give him some idea of what to do next. The silence served to reinforce the fact that no one was going to provide any information or any comfort again. He might as well be the last man left on earth.

Then he shouted at the sky in anger. "No, it isn't worth the price. Do you hear me? Do you hear me?" The tears were beginning to flow. The wind picked up suddenly as if in response to his lamentations. It howled a mournful sound as if it understood and was despairing Hunter's passing with his son.

Scott looked at the box that had been the source of his loss. "I better see what we got for the price of admission." He opened the box. It contained several small vials of a crystalline material that looked like it existed in both solid and liquid states. He started to put the box down but then he noticed that there was something else in with the vials.

What's this? He lifted the orb out of the box, put the box down, and turned the structure over in his hand. It looked like …a mapRock.

How can this be? We accounted for all the mapRocks and they worked. But, if this is part of the mapRock chain, it should not have worked. He put the mapRock back into the box. The silent loneliness began to wash over him again. The pain of his loss was almost crippling.

What do I do now? What can I do? This is the first time I have ever felt this alone. He absent-mindedly looked into the desert and saw that a vehicle was moving toward him at a high rate of speed, judging by the dust trail. He stood frozen watching the vehicle approach. Then his phone rang.

"Hi, Mom."

"Hi Scotty. I just wanted to let you know I was almost there."

"Where?" Then he remembered that LEAX had called her.

She answered, "Someone named LEAX called me and told me that you and dad were in danger and that I needed to come here as soon as possible." The word 'dad' cut into Scott's heart like a white-hot poker.

Scott took a moment to regain his composure and then told his mom, "I think I can see you. You should be a couple minutes from me right now. Pull into the turnout on top of the hill. I will meet you at the car."

"Can I talk to your dad?"

In a voice that spoke of incredible grief, he choked out the words that he still could not believe, "Dad is dead."

There was a silence between them and then Margie quietly said, "I was afraid of that from the beginning."

Margie pulled into the turnout, stopped the car, and sat there remembering their conversation in the kitchen less than a week ago. Scott ran up to her. They embraced sharing their loss.

Margie looked at Scott and managed a hoarse "How?"

"It's a long story, Mom. We should find some shade and sit down so we can talk."

Suddenly, a swirl of light appeared and a smallish figure materialized. It was an older individual wearing the same coat that LEAX had worn with the same eye structure that LEAX had.

"Who or what is that?" Margie asked, as she retreated behind Scott. Scott calmed his mom, walked over to the visitor, and stopped in front of him. They talked for a minute and then Scott brought him over to where his mom was.

"Mom, this is MERN. He is an Oent'rfazr. They're time travelers. Dad and I spent this journey with another Oent'rfazr named LEAX who..." and then he stopped. He couldn't finish the sentence.

Seeing Scott's discomfort, MERN began, "I am one of the Old Ones. Your husband was a brave man. The successful completion of this journey and his death represent something that is so significant and important that their total impact may never be understood but the continued existence of your world and my world owes everything to your husband and your son."

Margie was listening intently. "I don't understand."

"That is quite understandable. Hunter was a part of the last group of Oent'rfazr youth to be trained using the space ships that were the primary tool for our time travel for many years."

"Hunter was...an alien?" Margie couldn't believe what she was saying.

Scott nodded yes as if it would be more believable coming from him.

"Each youth was put into suspended animation and placed in a small flying craft and sent on a short journey to the past to understand our travel technology and to learn about other people and their times. Hunter was on his way to a town along the east coast of your country at the turn of the century. Something happened and his ship veered off course and crashed near a small town."

"Kecksburg," Scott said softly to his mom.

"The crash brought him out of suspended animation early and he was able to get out of the ship. He took cover in the woods when he heard all the noise and saw all the lights." Scott watched his mom as MERN easily explained the mystery that her husband had agonized over his entire life trying to unravel.

"Because there are so many things that could be discovered if an Oent'rfazr was captured, all trainees, during their final exercise, were given a treatment that overlaid the Oent'rfazr psyche with a human identity. That way, if he was discovered, he couldn't give himself away. In effect, your husband started becoming human that night."

Margie sat down in a daze.

"Under normal circumstances, the identity shell is removed within twenty-four hours to allow the Oent'rfazr personality to continue developing. In your husband's case, we couldn't get back to him. We had no experience with the shell existing more than twenty-four hours so we really didn't know what was going to happen.

"So, he was changed from an alien to a human then?"

"Not exactly. The human shell began to grow and thicken. As time passed, Hunt did become more and more human. From the time of the crash, Hunter was evolving as a human being and for all anyone knew, including him, he was a human being."

"But he was perfectly human in . . . Margie blushed . . .everything he did."

"When we were finally able to get back to him, it was decided to not interrupt what had become a classic life-species evolution experiment. Over time, however, the hardened human shell began to crack and he experienced pain from the contradiction resulting when the two personalities came in contact with each other and his Oent'rfazr knowledge was re-discovered."

"The headaches," Scott said.

"Had he continued, it's very possible that some morning he would have awakened as an Oent'rfazr and had no idea what or who he was and how he got there. It was then we decided to use him to locate the hidden technology before the B'stri found it."

"What technology and what's a B'stri?" Margie's voice began to show the strain of the day.

"The B'stri are a violent species of Oent'rfazr. LEAX, the third member of this journey, although physically and mentally an Oent'rfazr, was a passive, morphing B'stri disciple, who didn't complete his change until today. We didn't find out about the change in time to save either of them."

"Why did LEAX call me?"

"He told me that it was his intent to kill dad," Scott said, "and then to kill both of us because, as a family, we represented the major threat to the continued existence of the B'stri race."

Margie looked confused. "Why me? I wasn't a part of your journey?"

Dad told LEAX about your phone call —the one about finding solutions to the problems with the formulas that he used in the first time travel experiment.

Mern continued the conversation. "LEAX...the B'stri... extrapolated that you would be a critical part of the team that would find the technology and use it to displace the B'stri in the next phase of time travel experiments. Therefore, you had to be eliminated too. Hunter took care of the immediate issue but now we're faced with a new crisis that must be resolved if his loss isn't to be in vain."

Scott rubbed the back of his neck. "What do you mean in vain?"

"As you know, Scott, the information on how to use the technology was also hidden. Now that we have the technology that usage information has to be found. Your dad was going to be recruited for this next phase if he were successful. Now, we still have the problem but no solution...at least not yet."

"We talked about the possibility of my replacing my dad when we started the journey," Scott remembered, "but I ..."

"You have another reason to consider it now," MERN told him. "A reason besides your dad's death."

Scott looked at MERN not sure what he was talking about.

"I don't know if you thought about this, Scott, but you're part Oent'rfazr. You have a stake in both worlds. You got that from your father. You have shown a valuable understanding of Route 66 that may be needed again to find the technology notes. We need you to replace your father in the second half of the journey."

Margie gasped and all the pain of the last hour erupted in unbridled anger.

"I just lost my husband and now you're asking me to volunteer to lose my son and be happy about it? How dare you? You go straight *to hell* right now."

Scott gazed softly at his mom and then looked down for a long time.

"Do I have a choice in joining you or will it be like with my dad—join us or die?"

MERN answer was short. "I don't know."

"Why are you even thinking about this, Scott?"

Scott took his mom's hands, knowing she hadn't really understood his question. In a voice filled with understanding beyond his years, he said, "Just after dad made that very first trip into the future, we talked about its impact on mankind and on us. I remember he said he wondered whether he had created a caterpillar or a butterfly. He left me the opportunity to find the answer— to complete the challenge he didn't get a chance to fulfill."

There was a profound silence and then Margie looked at her son. "What now?"

"I guess we have two alternatives. Go back home and try to pick up our lives and go on from there."

"Or?"

"We can team up, as MERN noted, to finish the work dad started. What do you think?"

Before you decide, MERN said, "I need to tell you something that neither LEAX nor your dad knew."

Scott felt his muscles tense. "What now?"

"Your dad and LEAX were brothers. That was part of the reason they were paired. If you choose the journey, it's possible you may meet members of his family...your family."

Scott remembered his dad's comments and LEAX's comments about their lack of knowledge about their respective families.

Before Margie could comment, Scott noticed another long trail of dust twisting its way along the desert floor and up the side of the Black Mountains.

"It looks like someone else is in a big hurry to get here."

MERN stepped behand a nearby tree.

Scott and Margie stood at the top of Sitgreaves and shaded their eyes so they could follow the dust trail as it got closer and closer. A large black sedan with heavily tinted windows turned the last corner and came to a rolling stop in front of them. Scott looked at the vehicle and then nudged his mother.

"The plate." She nodded. A federal government plate. The sound of two doors opening and closing brought their focus back to the front of the car. Two men dressed in black suits, wearing sunglasses stepped onto the ground. Although she couldn't see their eyes, Margie felt the cold stares boring out from behind the sunglasses, incongruous under their jaunty Tyrolean hats.

"Do either of you know Hunter Johnson?

Margie stared at the two men. "Why do you want to know?"

The two men reached into their suit coats. Scott stepped in front of his mom. The two men flipped open wallets displaying silver gold badges that somehow didn't look like typical G-man badges.

"We are with the SAB."

Scott had never heard the term before. "What's the SAB?"

"Let's just say we're concerned with anything that might compromise the security of our country ...in *any* way." The emphasis on the word *any* left Scott with an empty feeling in his stomach.

That really sounds ominous.

The other man said, "Now, let me ask you, *again*."

Margie glared back at the men. "No, let me ask you *again*. Why do you want to know?" The two men turned their backs and began an animated discussion in tones that were too low to be heard.

They finally turned around. "Do you have some ID?"

Margie and Scott both gave them a look that demanded an answer. Why?

"Until we know exactly who you are, we cannot answer your questions."

Begrudgingly, both Margie and Scott located their IDs and gave them to the younger man.

Margie added, "This is all you get until you give *us* some answers."

One of the men took the IDs, went back to the sedan, and opened his phone. He talked, while looking at the IDs and then reached inside the car and pulled out two pieces of paper, which Scott could see were printed photos of each of them. The man closed the door, walked over to his partner, and showed him the photos. He nodded.

The man handed the ID cards back to them and said, "Thank you."

Taking a cue from his mom, Scott asked in a less than pleasant tone, "Now, can we get some answers?"

"The only thing we can tell you at this time is that the last group of astronauts to land on the moon found a number of papers with Dr. Johnson's signature on them hidden near the Tycho Brahe crater and in a cavern next to some very compelling evidence that life does exist on other planets. We need to find him to ask him how his name got there, if he's the one who put the papers there, when it happened, and did he have contact with any extraterrestrials?"

"Hunter is my husband."

Scott could tell his mom had decided not to tell them about his dad's death.

"Do you know where he is now, ma'am?"

Margie felt Scott give her a slight nudge. She nodded slightly.

"He was exploring out here and we were supposed to meet him but apparently we got our wires crossed."

"Can you call him?"

"I tried earlier but couldn't find him?"

"Would you mind trying now?"

Scott jumped in. "Let me see if I can get ahold of him, Mom." Scott opened his phone and dialed a number. He also discretely pushed a button to loop the call so it would ring through as if no one was answering the phone.

"No luck," Scott replied after a minute of ringing. The two men huddled again for several minutes.

"Okay, when he does contact you, we'd like you to have him give us a call." The request sounded more like a threat. One of the men handed Scott a card. It was a black card with the word 'SECURITY' and a single phone number. It had an area code that Scott had never seen before. On the back of the card were the white initials SEC.

The two men got into their car, sat there for a few moments, and pulled slowly out of the parking area.

"Let's see where they go," Scott told his mom.

The car stopped momentarily behind Margie's and Hunter's cars as if the two men were making notes on license plates and then started slowly down the road. After they got around the first corner, they stopped and waited.

Scott watched them and suggested, "I somehow don't think they believed us when we said we couldn't find dad. Something else must be going on. They made it too easy for us to see that they're waiting for us."

Margie looked at Scott in total amazement. "Dad's name on the moon? How did he do that? When did he do that?" Why didn't he tell us?"

MERN stepped out from his hiding place although Scott noticed he was keeping a tree between him and the feds. "I am leaving but think about what I said, both of you." Then he dissolved into the swirling blue mist.

The silence engulfed the two as they thought about what had just happened.

Then, from out of nowhere, a voice that sounded like it came from a long ways away said, "Take the box to the Topock Bridge in an hour."

Scott looked at his mom and shrugged his shoulders. "I guess we need to get to Topock to see what's going to happen next." As he leaned against the fender of his dad's car, he remembered the article he found in Oatman. There was something about it that stuck in his mind. He took the article out of his shirt pocket and started reading it to his mom.

"Johnson first to the future again. Three years ago, Dr. Hunter Johnson was the first human to astral project into the future. It started an incredible race among nations to duplicate the feat. Yesterday, three years after his historic first voyage, he did it again with a full body trip into the future that lasted forty-eight hours."

Scott stopped as he realized what the words were saying. He began searching for a publication date.

"Dad's first trip was six weeks ago not three years. How could he make a trip three years from now if he's...?"

Margie interrupted Scott, "That reminds me. Your father got mail this morning...from Kecksburg." She dug in her purse and handed Scott the letter.

He opened it, took out a sealed envelope, opened it, and began to read.

"Hunter, go back to the crash site and look in the large white oak tree. There's a piece of metal with a blue triangle and orange circle on it imbedded in the tree. Take the metal piece out and put it away so that no one knows you have it. It contains a record of your life before the crash. It's signed Hunt."

"How can that be?" Margie looked at her son.

"More added writing says,

The symbol also contains information about how to find the instructions for the technology. It's very important to keep it safe and tell no one until you find someone to help you read it. Dad signed the first note three days ago. He also signed the second note but with a different color of ink and printing style. There is no date other than it looks like the second note was written well after the first."

"A piece of metal with a blue triangle and orange circle," Margie repeated. She thought a minute. "The framed piece of metal Hunt kept by the phone?"

"Yes," Scott answered. "Although something is really strange here."

"What?" Margie responded.

"Dad told me about going back to Kecksburg a couple of days ago and leaving the first note but he didn't say anything about the second note or exactly what the symbol might contain." Margie took her son's hand.

"There's a lot about your father that we still don't know and that I need to know to help with my memory of him."

They walked to their cars and got in. Margie rolled her window down and said, "Topock?"

Scott moved stuff into the back seat and when he did, the list of words fell on the seat. He picked it up and looked at the last two words: '*death* and *Scott*'.

I wonder how much the person already knew about all this when he prepared this list?

Scott and his mom began the drive toward Topock. Scott looked in the rearview mirror, saw a cloud of dust forming behind them, and noted that the front end of the car emerging from that dust cloud belonged to a large black sedan.

Just then, Scott noticed a fuzzy brown caterpillar on the car window and he watched it trail slowly across the windshield moving its head from side to side as if looking for something.

"Caterpillar or butterfly? I guess we're both still looking for the answer to that question, little guy."

Secrets of the Oent'fazr, **the second book in the Oent'rfazr Dyad, begins with A New Journey.**

A New Journey

What had the voice said again? Scott tried to remember. *Meet on the Topock Bridge in an hour?* It had been a week full of surprises, disappointments, and sadness for everyone. Scott looked in the rearview mirror to make sure his mom was still close behind and not only saw her car but he also glimpsed the front end of the black sedan still following them in an incredibly amateurish manner.

They don't give up easily, Scott thought. The sign ahead read: Topock one mile. They were almost there.

I guess we will see what the next step in our journey is very soon. He looked in the back seat for the fifth time since leaving the Fishbowl to make sure the technology and the mapRock singularity found with it were still there. He wondered, *Will whatever they would find at Topock bring more understanding about what happened and about what they had to do to find the 'instructions'?* He finished that thought just as they drove up next to the old Topock Bridge. It had served the thousands of Route 66 travelers as they made their way across the Colorado River into California. Now old age and time had reduced it to a simple footbridge. Scott looked at the length of the bridge but didn't see anyone on either side. They parked their cars and walked over to the narrow gate that led onto the bridge.

"Mom, it looks like this is where we're supposed to be. Let's go find out why."

They started walking slowly toward the middle of the bridge.

"I don't see anything or anyone yet," Scott remarked. They reached the center of the bridge and stopped.

"What now?" Margie sounded and looked uncertain.

They stood there in silence for a few moments looking around. Scott opened his mouth to say something and then he saw it just several feet away from him. The familiar blue light swirling randomly on the footpath.

A figure began to materialize in the center of the light. Scott's facial expression changed from one of bewilderment to one of complete surprise and then unbounded joy.

It can't be he thought and then he almost shouted. "Dad, is it really you?" They embraced one another in a joyous bear hug. Scott had no words. Then, Scott stepped back to clear the way for his mom and dad to reconnect. After several minutes of watching his mom and dad, Scott could no longer contain himself.

Scott began impatiently, "What happened at the Fishbowl? I thought you were killed in the confrontation with LEAX. I saw you dissolve into thin air with my own eyes." How did you survive? Is LEAX still alive?" Hunter released Margie slightly to answer Scott.

"It's a long story that I want to share with you but first we need to shake the feds."

Scott looked around but couldn't see the sedan.

"How do you know about them? They didn't show up until after you and LEAX…left."

"There are a lot of things I found out about me, you, mom, LEAX, and the Oent'rfazr, while I was …gone but we need to find someplace quiet first."

Margie grabbed her husband's hand as they walked back to the where the cars were. "Where have you been? How did you get to the moon and when did you go? Why didn't you tell us? I am so happy to see you, sweetheart, I just can't stop talking." Hunter looked at Scott and raised his right eyebrow. Scott just laughed.

They got into their cars, drove into Topock, and found a restaurant hidden back away from the road. They got out, went in, and sat down at a booth away from the door.

Hunter began, "Scotty, do you remember what happened to me when I crash landed in Kecksburg and got left there?"

"Do you mean about the human shell that overlaid your Oent'rfazr personality?"

"Yes. It seems that when LEAX and I both touched the technology his body dissolved but it only destroyed my human shell leaving the real Oent'rfazr me almost intact. But that is another story."

"So, now you know your true identity, the one you have been looking for all your life, Dad?"

"Not quite. The long period of time when I existed as both species, a genetic anomaly developed within me." At the sound of those words, Scott cringed as he remembered that is how the B'stri came into being.

Hunter continued, "I kept the physical human form so that I look like I did but mentally I am equally human and Oent'rfazr —a first of a new race with hopefully the best of both species. I have a lot more to tell you but right now we have a lot of work cut out for us."

"What do you mean us?" Margie said

Hunter looked at them both. "I mean the first thing the three of us have to do is find a way to locate the instructions for the technology quickly or the Oent'rfazr, the B'stri, and the human race will become extinct.

Scott and Margie just stared at Hunter.

"Seeing the look on their faces, Hunter stopped and said, Come on, let's go home. "I really need some of your peanut butter casserole, Doris, and I think I may have a few surprises for you when we meet on the basketball court the next time, Scott." On the way, we can stop at the next site to see how and where we begin the second part of our journey and we can talk about the visits to the moon."

Scott looked puzzled. "The next site? We don't have any clues to even know where to begin to look."

"Do you remember the UFO cave?"

"Yeah," Scott responded.

"Do you remember what we found?"

"No, wait, yes. The numbers. Twenty-two something, something."

"Did they remind you of anything?" Scott thought for several moments and shook his head. "Actually I didn't really think about them after that night," Scott told his dad.

"What if you configure them to look like this?" Hunt showed Scott.

33.39.443 and -114. 39. 598?

Scott looked at the new configuration. "Nothing comes to mind. What are they?"

"I don't know and neither does anyone else."

"How about the ones who put created the clues or put the number there?"

"Do you remember LEAX telling us about the incredible potential of the technology and how the Oent'rfazr wanted to be sure it didn't fall into the hands of the B'stri?"

"Yes," Scott replied.

"They were so concerned that when they created the trail for our journeys each part was completed by a different Oent'rfazr at a different time and each mapRock was hidden by a different person at each site. None of the people involved talked to or even knew who the other people involved were. If we could find the particular Oent'rfazr who set-up the UFO site, he would have no idea what the numbers were. We three were the only people in the history of both races to see the Journey holistically. We have to repeat that discovery process to find the instructions."

"I will check my lap top to see if it has any suggestions."

"I would recommend that you look for things that link directly or indirectly with Route 66. It seems to be the common thread."

When they got back to the cars, Scott loaded the numbers into the laptop. While he was doing that, Hunter brought his wife up to date on things that happened on the journey.

Scott finished checking and told his mom and dad, "It looks like those numbers could be a computer coding reference, a variant of an Ottendorf cypher, or a latitude and longitude reference."

"That is an interesting combination. It appears the first two will have to be deciphered based on finding other information, which will take time. We can divide the research among ourselves to make it go faster. The latitude longitude idea though could be checked rather quickly as it would seem to just identify the physical location of some place we need to go. That something may just be another clue but it's a start."

"Let me see what I can find," Scott began. "The first two numbers in each set are 33 and minus 114. That is 33 degrees north of the equator and 114 degrees west of the prime meridian. That puts it in Arizona somewhere between the Mexico border and the area south of Wickenburg and west of Prescott and east of the California border."

"That is nowhere near any part of Route 66," Hunter said.

"The minutes indicate that it's near Interstate 10 closer to the California border than to Prescott. Let me plug in the seconds. It looks like the site is right outside of Quartzite."

"Quartzite? The small town that caters to winter vacationers and recreationalists? Nice place to visit but there's nothing at Quartzsite that could have *any* connection to Route 66."